His Heart's Burden

A LETTING LOVE IN PREQUEL STORY
BOOK 0.5

DAWN BACA

To my husband Jeremy,

You are my real life hero. Your strength of character, and incredibly deep sense of honor is what made fall in love with you from the very beginning.

To my 'Uncle' Earl Gates,

You always supported my love of reading in every way. Encouraging my thirst for knowledge. I owe so much of that to you. I never told you how sorry I was, and it hurts that I never got to say goodbye.
Losing you left a hole in my heart.

To every person who has ever had to slay dragons to be present for your child. Your courage and perseverence has not gone unnoticed. You are a shining example of what all parents should strive to be. Your efforts are appreciated.

Difficult roads often lead to beautiful destinations.
— *Anonymous*

CHAPTER 1

The Choice

Eli

Eli Tetrick stood paralyzed in the kitchen of his small two-bedroom apartment. The silence was suffocating. He felt trapped, as if someone had buried him alive. His body was numb, his heart was racing painfully, and he felt like he was going to die. It certainly felt like he was dead inside. It was as if he had no emotion left.

He had been barely functioning the last two weeks. Dazed, just going through the motions on autopilot. He'd lost weight. The guys at the shop had noticed and teased him about being on one of the new kale diets or ginger cleanses or whatever this week's latest trend was. He didn't care. He didn't care about anything anymore. But they were right. In a sense. It was a diet, though not one that he would ever recommend.

The joke about the *Divorce Diet* was real. Eli was experiencing it firsthand. In a single moment, a gut punch changed everything as he knew it. His world had turned upside down, and he could barely move with the giant boulder sitting in the pit of his stomach. Every thought left him feeling like he was drowning, struggling to keep his head above the proverbial water. If his lungs had refused to do their job on their own without his input, he'd have stopped breathing a long time ago. Just like eating. Or well, in his case, the lack thereof. He wasn't intentionally starving himself. He simply wasn't hungry. Not in the slightest. And the few times he'd tried to "fake" it, he'd only chucked it up later. Not exactly on his list of favorite experiences, so he just lived on a couple of cheese sticks and a beer before crashing onto the couch. Ironically, he drank the beer to create the impression that he had come home drunk and passed out, so he'd be left alone without having to explain himself.

Not that he slept. He didn't do that either. His

mind wouldn't stop churning. The *how's*. The *why's*. The endless questions, the internal recriminations. He had those down in spades.

He was such an idiot!

But there would be hell to pay if he didn't come home.

His wife. God, how that word stuck in his craw.

He forced his mind to rephrase the sentence. His soon to be ex-wife, even that didn't soothe the demons in his chest, none-the-less, Tandy would have pitched a fit and he didn't have the energy to fight with her. And under the circumstances, there was zero doubt in his mind if he saw her face, if she opened her mouth and said a single word, the dam would break, and all the hurt, anger, disgust with himself would spill. He wouldn't have been able to keep his mouth clamped tightly shut, considering all the secrets he stored in the box under the stone in his gut. He'd have spewed all the ugliness out until he was empty. That wouldn't do anyone any good. Especially his children.

That said, he'd come home late every night for the past two weeks, ever since he received the envelope that changed the outcome of his life. He couldn't bring himself to come home until he could guarantee everyone was dead asleep.

He'd had to force himself to follow this practice after he'd discovered her dirty little secret.

After a much-needed shower, he'd kissed his girls' foreheads, and tucked them a little tighter under their covers, their precious bears next to them leaving a little of his presence for them to know he loved them. Then, sliding under the blanket on the couch, he waited with bated breath in the dark for his alarm to go off at four in the morning, allowing him to escape the house before Tandy or the girls woke.

He chastised himself for being a coward, but two years of fighting with his wife left him drained. Tandy had played him better than any country fiddle. He couldn't make her happy. He'd been so naïve to think he could. They'd barely known each other before she'd come to him pregnant.

From there, his strict Southern Baptist upbringing kicked in. Her blue-blooded, southern belle family hadn't helped, that was for sure. Daughters of the Confederacy did *not* have children out of wedlock. He'd been informed that such an unthinkable thing would send her great-great grandmama into the vapors from her grave.

Considering so many marriages of the semi-aristocratic families of the Old South were preapproved matches made without taking personal compatibility or love into the equation, they wed as they were told, and figured it out later. His situation wasn't much different.

While he wasn't ready to be a husband or a father, he'd had no choice once his folks heard the news. He had accepted that this was common, and he'd married her, hoping that they would fall in love as they became a family. He'd stepped up and done the "right" thing before his daughter Savannah was born. Addison had been born just a year later. Irish twins, they called it. Hell, he wasn't even Irish. Not that it mattered.

Thinking of Savi, his beautiful little spitfire, his gut clenched, and he sucked in a breath. She had wrapped her tiny little fingers around his heart the moment they placed her in his arms, after she was born. His daughters were his entire world. He'd always thought he could protect their little bubble, keeping the real world out of their purview. Until two weeks ago, he'd planned to remain in his love-less, soulless marriage for the sake of his girls for years to come. He had thought he was so smart. That he was handling it well, all things considered. How wrong he'd been. About everything. For so, so long.

Eli flopped onto a chair at the kitchen table. The rickety chair wobbled beneath him. His fist clenched. The heavy, thick envelopes within poked into his palm. It snapped him out of his morose musings. Looking down at the two envelopes, now noticeably crinkled in his hand as though it was a snake waiting to strike him, he tossed the envelopes onto the small, cheap Formica dinette. In the still room, they landed on the flat surface with such a force that he flinched. The paper hit the table and ricocheted with the reverberations as if someone had been slapped.

The breath he hadn't even realized he'd been holding rushed out. Blinking back the tears that he refused to shed, he leaned down and snapped up his gym bag. Gripping it in his sweaty palm, he stood and stalked out of his apartment for the last time.

Eli didn't bother looking back.

CHAPTER 2

Stupid Is As Stupid Does

SIX MONTHS LATER

Eli

Eli sat next to Thean at the old run-down dive bar that sat neglected around the corner from the shop. He'd been sucking it up, doing his best to not say anything out loud to anyone outside of his family, lawyer, or his ex. The guys at the garage knew something was up. But other than the usual joshing about his weight loss, and growing baggage under his eyes, they'd respected his silence.

The latest Tandy drama had taken a huge toll on him. He was unraveling at the seams.

"I needed this," he said. His voice was low, his fingers tightened on his beer.

"What's up?" Thean asked. He side-eyed Eli while smashing the peanut husks against the bar top.

Eli stared at the TV screen across the bar. He wasn't watching the game. His eyes were too glassed over to see it, anyway.

"I fucked up. Bad. I'm so stupid."

Thean set his bottle of beer down and swiveled his bar stool to face Eli head on.

"Hey, it can't be that big a deal."

"Thean, I'm never going to see my daughter again. Rushing in, I failed to consider the conse-quences, and more than that, I never expected Tandy could be so cruel."

"Wait, I thought you had two girls?"

"Yeah. So, did I. Until I didn't."

Eli downed the rest of his beer and motioned for the bartender. A tall, super skinny, unnatural blonde came over and dropped off two more bottles of beer in front of them.

Eli cast a look around, the small electric candles on the tables setting off gloomy, dancing shadows in their wake. The atmosphere was quiet, almost menacing. There were only a handful of people in the bar at the moment. He didn't really notice much of his surroundings at all, he just needed a minute to push down the bile threatening to rise from his churning gut.

"I'm confused. The last time your wife came in bitching at you, she brought the girls, and both called you daddy."

Eli hung his head as the shame flooded through him.

"It's complicated. When Tandy said she was pregnant, I didn't question it. I never thought I needed to, even if I'd only known her a few months. We hadn't been careful. And well. Yeah."

Thean smirked.

Eli shrugged. He wasn't the first college kid to let his dick lead where his brain would've feared to tread. Hormonal boys being stupid was a tale as old as time.

"We rushed to the altar. A few months after Savannah was born, Tandy became pregnant with Addison. The girls are a year apart. I was only working at the shop part-time. I dropped out of school to work. Even though that only pissed her and her parents off."

"But I thought you were basically happy, though?"

Eli looked his friend in the eye. At least out of everything, this was something he could speak to with a certain begrudging clarity.

"Honestly. No. I don't think we've ever been happy together. I think Tandy had an idea in her head of what a respectable husband looked like and her parents approved of. Money, to not have to work, keep up with the Joneses, vacations, etc. The life she'd grown up with and grown accustomed to."

Eyes wide, Thean nodded understandingly.

"I'm not the white collar, six-figure manager somewhere. I'm just a low-income grease monkey. And she resents that."

"Shit, man." Thean set the bottle on the bar with a thump, hard enough to vibrate Eli's empty bottle.

"Anyway, it doesn't matter now. Tandy's been having an affair. She's involved with an ex-boyfriend. Something crawled in my brain and kept nagging me that Addison wasn't mine."

Thean stared at him, his mouth gaping.

"It kept eating at me. Finally, after catching her on the phone with him, unknowingly, I sent in samples, just to be sure. I figured if I was wrong, I would put a stop to the affair and leave the rest alone. I just wanted to clear my suspicions about Addison. It came as a shock to learn Savannah wasn't mine. I included her sample as an afterthought, nothing more. I had never questioned her paternity."

"Fuck dude."

"I adore Savannah. She's still my daughter in my heart. But, standing there with the results in my hand, it was obvious Tandy lied about everything to get me to marry her."

Eli flinched as he remembered the morning he woke up in the woods, sicker than a dog after he'd seen the truth. He intentionally went off grid to avoid her. The hangover that followed his three-day bender had been hell. It wasn't exactly the most adult way to handle her betrayal, but in deference to himself, he hadn't exactly been in his right mind at the time either.

The bartender stopped by their spot. "Can I get you another round?"

He looked at his empty bottle, surprised. "Yes, please."

Thean nodded. She walked away.

The bartender set down their drinks and cleared away the empties.

Eli picked up the story where he'd left off. "I couldn't think straight. I went to a lawyer and had the papers drawn. Then left the paternity test and the divorce papers on the kitchen table." He took another deep drink and choked.

"How did she take it when confronted by the evidence?" Thean's brow arched.

"At that point, I didn't want to talk to Tandy or to work it out. I didn't see the need for further explanations or excuses. I just walked away, not stopping to think of the damage it might do to the girls."

"I bet that didn't go over well."

"Didn't give myself a chance to think about it. I was numb."

"That's rough, man."

"Looking back, I regret not taking a step back and thinking it through. Chalk it up to another stupid decision, being so rash. We've paid dearly for it, the girls especially, but I'm not sure it would have changed much. I couldn't stay married to her. But... Maybe if I hadn't left the way I did, she wouldn't be as volatile as she is now."

"Why the hell is she angry? She's the one screwing around."

"With Tandy, I've discovered the worse the lies are, the harder she tries to redirect the blame. No one wins, least of all the girls." Eli rubbed his thumb around the condensation on his bottleneck.

"I wish it hadn't gotten so ugly, for the girls' sake." He glanced over his shoulder when the door slammed against the frame. Someone else had come in, probably looking to drown his sorrows too.

Thean's hands clenched around his bottle, his shoulders tense.

Eli stretched his neck. It was so stiff. The sleepless nights on a sofa at the shop were getting to him. He wasn't sure if he should spill all the details. It wasn't in his nature to air his dirty laundry, which is why he'd kept it quiet the last few months.

"In what way?" Thean asked.

"Tandy saw red. My leaving her was an insult to her. Since I was only ordered to pay support for Addison, in order to stick it to me, she made up non-existent expenses, like child care, to supplement it."

"Why?"

"There's a set amount calculated based on the

number of children, custody terms, and incomes of the parents."

"Did she argue about Savannah?"

"The judge had a copy of the paternity tests right there in black and white."

"Ouch." Thean's jaw clenched.

"Her response was, since I didn't have to support Savannah, I shouldn't get visitation of her, and the judge agreed."

"That's fucked up, man!"

"It blindsided me, to be honest. I hadn't even considered that as a possibility. And even when I explained to the judge that I was the only father Savannah had known, it didn't matter one iota. Proof was proof. I wanted to kick myself, for being thick-headed, standing there dumbstruck at the judge's decision. I was angry about all her manipulations. It never dawned on me she'd be spiteful—so spiteful that she would cut me off from Savannah."

"I'm so sorry."

"The only father Savannah knows, now I'm gone. She can't come when I pick up Addison. The look of bewilderment and hurt, like I don't care, kills me very time."

"Can't you reason with Tandy?"

"I've tried. But I can't get through to her. I

swear the look she gave me in court that day was one of triumph. It was like she gloated that I may have won a single skirmish, but she'd won the whole damn battle, and relished the pain it caused me." He chugged his beer.

"She wants you back," Thean said. "I saw that much."

"She doesn't know what she wants, but more than that, she's still seeing her ex, though I'm sure her parents don't know. They aren't fond of Luke. Hell, they keep calling me, telling me it's my duty to stay with my family."

"So, enlighten them. It's about time they knew the truth and quit putting you on the spot as the bad guy."

"With her family, it wouldn't make a difference. Stiff upper lip. Don't make waves. The southern elite could give the British royalty some tips."

"That's some serious screwed up shit man. No wonder you've been a wreck. We've all noticed it, but damn, we didn't know shit was this bad. I'm sorry to hear."

"I married her trying to do the right thing. I didn't realize how little I knew her, or her motivations, until it was too damn late."

"Where do you go from here?" Thean asked.

"I don't fucking know. I dug the hole, now I've got to lie in it. Tandy is punishing me for leaving her."

He hoped he didn't sound as desperate as he felt.

"Sorry you're going through this shit. But I'm here when you need a beer and to vent." Thean pursed his lips and clinked his bottle to Eli's.

CHAPTER 3

Fresh Starts

Cassie

C assandra Flynn stared out the window. The beautiful courtyard below her fourth-floor office was damp from the rain. Since moving to Durham, her body felt far older than her twenty-four years. She used to thrive at work, but the ridiculous pace of her new job was quickly wearing her out.

Her three months in North Carolina had been exhausting. An unrelenting fatigue made her question the decision to move. Cassie never expected corporate event planning to be more stressful than being a travel agent.

A soft knock sounded as the door opened. Her office sidekick, Enaria, peeked in with a smile. The older woman, with her plump cheeks and motherly heart, had taken her under her wing from the first day she'd arrived. Her wavy chestnut hair desperately tried to escape the twisted knot she'd started the day with.

"Are you ready to head out?"

"I thought you'd never ask," Cassie sighed.

"You sound exhausted. I hope they aren't working you too hard."

"I'm beating down the learning curve one day at a time." Cassie exhaled another deep breath.

"I'd hate to see you scared off before the fun begins." Enaria laughed. Her voice had gained a musical lilt from the years she spent in England with her British pilot husband.

Cassie stacked up the files scattered across her desk and slid them into the last drawer of her file cabinet. She locked it, grabbed her purse, and joined her friend at the door.

Downstairs in the parking lot, Enaria snickered at Cassie's car.

"Hi, Morris."

"Be nice to the little guy."

Cassie patted the worn vinyl top of the minis-cule British sports car she'd had since high school.

"I can't believe an American would buy one of those on purpose. Imagine driving it in the snow." Enaria smirked, shaking her head. She walked over and unlocked the large Chevrolet parked across from Cassie's. It was easily twice the size of Cassie's convertible.

Faced with a limited budget, Cassie's options had been slim. She'd been smitten with the used little blue MG Midget at first sight. Even if her parents had tried to talk her out of it, saying it was a hunk of junk that would be nothing but problems. They hadn't been wrong, but between infatuated youth, and the sale price, she'd dived in head first.

Cassie put the key in the ignition and turned it. There was a muted click, followed by an ominous silence.

"Damn it." She slapped the steering wheel.

Her friend's musical laughter filled the air as she walked over and leaned against the front of the MG.

"Morris giving you a hard time again?"

She ignored her friend's teasing. "I'll need a jump."

Enaria hid her grin behind her hand.

Cassie called her AAA road service, then leaned against the door facing her friend's humored gaze. At least it wasn't raining or snowing. North Carolina's winters were far colder than those in Florida, making her question leaving her childhood home, where the weather was warm and the beaches welcoming. And most of all, her car was practical.

"Want to get a drink after this?" Enaria asked.

"I'll need one."

Twenty minutes later, the tow truck operator stood by her car, shaking his head. He couldn't get it started, either.

"Want to try the shop Finn uses?"

"Might as well. I have to send it somewhere," Cassie muttered.

Enaria handed over a business card for Vintage British. Enaria's husband, Finn, had his own classic British car and knew the best mechanic. And of course, Enaria was all too familiar with the expenses that came with them, which was why she mocked Morris every chance she got. They followed the tow truck to Vintage British, and Enaria introduced Cassie to Thean as he came out of the shop.

Thean was young, tall, and lanky, with just the right amount of muscles under his black t-shirt to make him sexy. For someone who worked on cars, he was certainly cleaner than she expected.

Cassie glanced around the small, comfortable shop. It even smelled sweet. A citrus aroma filled the air.

Thean took a quick peek under the hood, then glanced up at Cassie. "I'll need to keep it overnight."

Cassie let out a heavy breath. "Should I even ask what this will cost me?"

"Guess you weren't prepared for the reality of British cars, eh?" Thean laughed.

"I've learned some lessons along the way. Like using metric, instead of a standard wrench, prevents an expensive disaster." Cassie laughed.

Thean looked away, pinched the bridge of his nose, and let out a harrumph. He cocked his head and said with a hint of derision she didn't appreciate, "So, you bought a quirky car, knowing nothing about it." He let out another hearty laugh.

Cassie shrugged. What could she say?

Enaria turned her head away. Her shoulders shook.

Thean laughed even harder.

Cassie shook her head. "I can't help it if I fell in love with it. Or that I got it cheap."

"You've got a nice car. They're just finicky," Thean said.

"I've been told that before."

"Leave your car with me. We'll take care of it for you." Thean reached his hand out and smiled.

Cassie got her car back the next day.

It had been a simple fix, a crimped wire draining the battery. But a few weeks later, it wouldn't start again.

At the shop, she and Enaria stood off to the side of the reception desk, waiting for the mechanic. Thean came in through the side door and handed the keys to Cassie.

"The solenoid was bad," he said, as he handed her the invoice.

Glancing down, she let out a sigh of relief. She had expected it to cost much more, considering what past visits had run.

A tall, dark-haired man wearing fitted jeans and a plain black T-shirt walked in from the back room and nodded at them.

"Hi Enaria, how's Finn?" The man asked.

"He's good," she said.

"And the roadster?" he asked.

Enaria rolled her eyes. "It's still British."

Everyone chuckled. Enaria's feelings on persnickety British cars were not a secret.

Thean smiled. "Cassie, I'd like to introduce you to the manager, Eli Tetrick."

He was younger than she expected for a manager of such a high-end specialty car shop.

"Ah, so you're the owner of the Midget Thean mentioned." Eli smiled as he stretched his hand over the counter to shake hers.

Heat rose in her cheeks despite her efforts to thwart it. She shook his hand, marking the size and warmth of his calloused palm.

"It wasn't bad, I promise."

Cassie's blush deepened. He must think she was ridiculous.

"It's not every day we see one of these guys. But it suits you."

"You make it sound like I'm crazy."

"It's a compliment, I promise." He gave her a wink.

The way his eyes lit up and the charming, lopsided grin made her pulse speed up.

A tongue-tied Cassie turned her face away.

Enaria stared all googly eyed at Eli as though she wasn't already a happily married woman.

After thanking Eli and Thean, they left.

Her friend pounced on her as they reached the parking lot.

"That man is like a tall drink of icy cold spring water on a hot summer day," she gushed.

"Which one?" Cassie asked.

"Eli, silly. You should go out with him."

"If you think he's so hot, you go out with him."

Enaria scowled, wiggling her left hand with her sparkling wedding ring. "Why not try to get to know him?"

"He's not my type." She typically went for the corporate suit type. "And I doubt I'm his." Tall, leggy, athletic blondes probably surrounded Eli.

"You sound like an office snob. Finn thinks he's a great guy. Finn's known Eli for years. I heard he went through a rough divorce a while ago." She sighed as she opened her car door.

Cassie slid into the little convertible, the top down, and looked over at her friend. "He's cute, I'll give you that." She waved her hand in the air nonchalantly. She wasn't in the market for a new boyfriend. Then again, her friend was right. The man exudes sex appeal. And he'd made her blush.

Not that she would admit that to Enaria. "I'll think about it."

Enaria beamed.

Despite pretending indifference, she wondered why he had divorced, and how long ago it had happened.

THE NEXT MORNING, CASSIE SAT AT HER DESK, staring blurry-eyed at a pile of papers. She looked up from them as Enaria popped her head in through the open door.

"Grab a cup of coffee with me?" Enaria had a cheesy grin on her face.

Cassie nodded and got up from her desk, grabbing her coffee mug. They walked down the hall to the break room. The twelve-hour days were taking their toll again.

"He asked about you," Enaria said. Her attention remained on the brewing coffee.

"Who?" Cassie asked.

Enaria laughed. "Eli, silly. Finn ran into him yesterday, and Eli asked about you."

Cassie focused on reaching for the creamer across the counter.

"He wanted to know if you were single. And what Finn thought about him asking you out."

Did she seem so desperate that her friend's husband felt the need to act as a matchmaker? She hated herself for wanting to know, but she had to ask. "What did Finn say?"

"He gave him your number and told him to call you."

Cassie groaned decidedly, ignoring the flutter in her stomach.

CHAPTER 4

Jumping In

Cassie

Cassie was staring at her computer, glaring at an email, when Eli phoned her office. It had been a couple of days since she'd seen him last.

"I hoped to convince you to have a drink with me tomorrow, or maybe lunch?"

There was an awkward pause for a moment before she responded. "Sure, drinks sound good. Let's meet at the Hot Rod Grille." It was around the corner from her apartment, which made it a simple choice.

"See you there about seven," he said.

"Let's make it seven-thirty."

"Seven-thirty then," he agreed.

Cassie stared at the phone in her hand long after he'd hung up.

She was nearly late getting to the Grille, having torn through her closet in search of a suitable outfit, telling herself all the while the date with Eli wasn't important. Settling on a loose, silky blouse in a dove grey that matched her eyes and a pair of black jeans, she was glad she made the effort when she saw Eli.

He wore perfectly pressed dark pants and a blue button-down shirt, his brown hair brushed into submission. An altogether appealing package.

They sat at the bar, shelled, and ate peanuts and drank beer, chased by the occasional shot of tequila. Cassie didn't make a habit of drinking on work nights, and she hadn't meant to drink a lot tonight. But she was having a wonderful time and lost count of how many glasses she'd emptied. Eli was fun to be around, with his witty banter and straightforward manner. They kept the conversation light, talking about her MG and his love of British classic cars. They didn't touch on any personal topics which kept the atmosphere light. She was glad she came. It had been such a long time since she'd been on a date.

"I don't think we should have had that last beer," she said. Her head felt like it was underwater.

Eli hiccupped. "More like the last three."

"Hmm…" she stood, the suddenness of the movement making her weave, and she gripped the edge of the counter.

"Need help?"

"If I'm not back in five minutes, drag me out," she said with a laugh.

He grinned in response.

She returned a few minutes later, and Eli signaled for the tab.

After he'd settled the bill, they played rock, paper, scissors to see if they should walk or call a cab. Cassie won, and so they walked the block and a half to her apartment. Eli supported her as her legs wobbled like jelly. They stumbled up two flights of stairs while she giggled, on the verge of hysterics.

Taking the keys from her, he propped her against the wrought iron banister across from her front door, and she watched him fumble with the key in the lock. Her inhibitions gone, she leaned in and kissed the back of his neck. It wasn't her habit to be so forward, but it had been months since she'd felt the arms of a man around her and hot lips on hers. He turned to her, burying his hands in her hair, returning her kisses with an unexpected passion. The unlocked door swung wide, and they hobbled to the couch with lips locked and limbs entangled.

Cassie struggled to keep her senses together. A slight movement to the side of her caught her eye. She noted the wide, open door. A few feet away, her long-haired Calico sat on the entertainment center. Seshat, named after the Egyptian goddess of wisdom, gave them a disinterested stare, and then turned curious eyes to the open door.

"The cat!" Cassie cried.

Eli was too busy kissing her neck to respond.

"The cat!" she repeated with more force as she tried to push at his arm.

Eli remained oblivious to her plight, instead fixated on his struggle to unclasp her bra.

"The door," she spat as she pushed on his chest. "The door is open!"

Peering at her, he climbed off the couch, stumbled over, and slammed the door with his foot. She stood to face him, grasping his hand to keep from swaying, and kissed him again. In fact, she was still kissing him as she dragged him to her bedroom.

She flicked her shirt aside, unclasped her bra, and let it drop to the floor.

Clearly impatient, Eli fought to remove his shoes.

Kicking her silver sandals into the closet, she wriggled to drag her skin-tight jeans off. The fabric clinging to every inch of her; she gasped for air as she tossed them with the rest of her clothes in a heap on the floor.

Their mouths met again, tongues tangling as she worked her hands beneath his shirt to touch his firm flesh. Frustrated by the need to tear her mouth away from his, she yanked the fabric over his head, and again took possession of his lips, mashing his nose. The dimly lit room made her bold.

Moonlight filtered through the cracks of the closed blinds, showering faint light onto their semi-naked bodies. They fell onto her bed, arms wrapped around each other, and lips locked in a battle of tongues. He smelled of citrus and a warm woodsy cologne she couldn't place. His back was slick with sweat. Tequila, beer, and salt coated his lips. She ran her fingers through his hair and gripped his shoulders.

Cupping her face with his callused hands, he kissed her. His passion reached deep into her soul, and the energy between them was far stronger than Cassie expected. No longer urgent, his lovemaking turned tender. He caressed each spot with feather light kisses as his fingers stroked her skin in gentle, circular motions. When he finally entered her, the experience was intense, like riding a wave cascading from the sea.

THE NEXT MORNING, SHE AWOKE ALONE. SHE wrestled with the sheets twisted around her legs. A soft breeze from the barely open window fluttered over her uncovered breasts. She groaned. She hadn't behaved with such reckless disregard in a long time. Seshat slept among the blankets on the floor.

The sun, peeking through her blinds, filled the room with a soft golden glow. She rolled out of bed. Her head felt like there were boxers inside, fighting to get out. She threw on a t-shirt and a pair of yoga pants and ambled into the kitchen with the cat on her heels. Eli was leaning against the counter with a full cup of steaming coffee. A fresh pot stationed behind him, hot and ready. He looked even better in the soft morning light than he had the night before. She didn't think it possible for him to be any sexier.

Purring loudly, Seshat hurried over to her bowl in the corner.

"Good morning," he mumbled without looking her in the eye.

"Ugh. Not yet." She rubbed her temples. "I could use an aspirin. You?"

"Please." He poured a second cup of coffee and handed it to her.

"This is a godsend." The aroma filled her nostrils.

Reaching into the cupboard, she pulled a bottle of generic aspirin out, and showed him the bottle. "Is this okay?" He nodded, and she poured a couple of pills into her hand, handing them to him before pouring a few more out for herself.

"Are you upset with me?" Eli asked, looking everywhere around her, his gaze never landing on her.

"Why on earth would I be upset?"

"Would you have slept with me if you were sober?"

"Ask me when I'm sober." She tried to keep a straight face but couldn't pull it off.

His shoulders relaxed, and he grinned back at her.

They bantered for a few minutes over the coffee before chagrin flushed his face.

"I've looked around, and I can't find my keys anywhere. I must have dropped them on the grass when we stumbled around," he said.

"Let me grab my shoes and I'll help you look," Cassie said.

He opened the front door and hesitated. Cassie followed his gaze to the bunch of keys spread out on the mat. "I meant to do that," he said.

Heat flooded her cheeks as she ogled his firm butt when he stooped to pick them up. "Hoping someone will steal your car?"

Eli pointed to the door with a smug expression. A key hung from the doorknob, attached to a chain dangling with others.

"Touché." Cassie snorted. She was glad her roommate Hank was out of town. It would have been awkward having to explain last night to him.

Stuffing his keys in his back pocket, he smiled. "I'm going to call a cab to take me to get my car. Do you want me to bring yours back?"

Startled, she wasn't expecting such a selfless

gesture. "Thank you, but I'll do the same after I shower."

He glanced down at his watch. "It's only six-thirty. There's time if you want to share the cab."

"That would be great. Give me fifteen minutes."

Eli's brow rose, but he didn't say a word.

"Trust me. Fifteen minutes." She raced out of the front room. Stripping as she moved, she stepped into the shower without waiting for the water to warm.

Holy shit!

The freezing water beating the top of her head made her tremble. There wasn't time to waste waiting for the temperature to be comfortable. Dumping a handful of shampoo in her hand, she quickly lathered her hair, then stood under the icy spray, rinsing it away as she scrubbed her body. Satisfied she'd removed the soap; she flipped the water off and jumped out of the shower. With her hair dripping down her back, she dried her body off before hastily wrapping the towel around her head. Without looking at the colors, she jerked on her underwear before yanking a pair of jeans from the dresser, then stuffing her legs into the holes as she hopped around for balance. She lay flat on the bed and snapped them closed. Shaking the towel from her head, it hit the floor in a wet pile. In the closet, she pulled out the first sweater she saw and yanked it on. She ran a brush through her tangled mass of hair, twisting it into a messy bun on her head before searching for her boots.

Pulling them on over her jeans, she shut the lights off and walked down the hall to the kitchen.

The clock on the microwave told her it had taken her twelve minutes to get ready.

"I'm impressed." Eli gave her a once over as a wide grin filled his face.

She nodded, grabbed her keys and purse off the counter, and waited at the door. They reached the street just as the cab pulled up to the apartment complex.

At the pub, Eli leaned in and gave her an awkward peck before he got into his car. He waved as he pulled out of the parking lot, leaving her standing there staring at his taillights.

A WEEK LATER, CASSIE MADE AN IMPROMPTU VISIT to the shop, hoping to see Eli. They'd talked every day on the phone, but this was the first time she had seen him since their night together. Leaning against the desk on the other side of the counter, he had his back to the room, listening to someone on the phone. He was trying to smooth the ruffled feathers of a disgruntled customer; they could hear hollering through the receiver. He held the phone away from his ear while scribbling on a notepad.

Thean leaned over and whispered. "It's an important client, but he's a drama queen and only Eli can manage him." He walked her to the far edge of the room by the water cooler.

Cassie nodded and chatted with him about her car, acting up again while she waited for Eli to notice her. He looked up at her and smiled, held up his hand, fingers spread out, showing he needed five minutes.

"I sympathize about the sticker shock," Eli said, focusing on his customer.

Thean rolled his eyes.

She rubbed her arms as the stone walls gave off a chill. The customer's agitated voice carried. She could hear him from across the room.

"Your prices are ridiculous."

"Not for repairs on an Aston Martin Zagato replica."

"Humph."

"It was almost totaled when it arrived," Eli reminded the customer.

The voice responded in a huff. "I am aware of what my son has done. Damn seventeen-year-olds."

Eli looked her way again, and she gave him a sympathetic smile, her heart lifting as his face softened in response. He leaned further away from the earpiece to escape the full brunt of the rant.

"—gouged over this repair," the man on the phone snapped.

"There is another qualified repair shop in Charlotte," Eli replied.

Charlotte was almost two hundred miles away.

"Fine, I'll sign off on the damn repairs," the voice growled through the phone.

"Thank you, sir. I'll order the parts and get to work right away." Eli winked at her and ended the call.

The butterflies in her stomach fluttered as he rose and stepped away from the desk.

Before he reached her, a car squealed into the lot, and a tall, willowy woman with long, straight, ebony hair got out and stormed into the waiting area. The woman stared at Eli, and then her gaze flew over to Cassie.

She exploded. "Are you the one he's sleeping with?"

What the hell? Cassie's mouth dropped. Her shoulders tensed.

The woman took a step in her direction. Her face twisted in rage. "I asked a simple question. Are you sleeping with my husband?"

She was now inches from Cassie's face, and the spittle was flying faster than her words.

"Whoa, calm down, Tandy." Eli glared at her as his back stiffened.

Thean's face turned pink, and he made a hasty exit.

Cassie wished she had been fast enough to join him when Eli gave her a look full of apology, his mouth a rueful twist, and his eyes dark with emotion.

"What do you want?" he asked.

"I want to know if she's the reason you missed dinner last night with your family." Her voice held the air of a petulant child.

Cassie's stomach dropped, her hands growing clammy. *He was divorced. Wasn't he?* Yet the angry woman was acting like they weren't. Cassie turned to leave.

Eli drew himself up, and said in a strong, no-nonsense tone, "First, don't you dare barge into the shop and yell at my customers. Second, you and I are not a family. Divorce means it's over whether or not you accept it."

The woman had her own agenda, because she took a step closer, jabbing her finger into Eli's chest.

"The girls missed you. I told them you were coming. You owe it to the girls. Just because we're divorced doesn't give you the right to ignore them."

Eli swatted her hand away, then took a step closer, slapping his hands on his hips. "I won't tell you again. Stop making promises you can't keep. It confuses the girls. You and I are done. Your behavior here is exactly why we aren't together. I will not allow you to manipulate me any longer." His tone was calmer than he appeared, his features taut with a splash of color in his cheeks.

"Well, if you won't be there for them, then I don't know what I'll do." Her face scrunched and her eyes narrowed. Tandy crossed her arms over her chest.

Cassie shrank back to be less conspicuous, anything to prevent the irate woman's wrath from returning to her. She stood as still as possible and kept her focus on a chip in the tile floor.

"Addison is my responsibility. Are you going to go screaming at Luke on Savannah's behalf?"

"But—"

"But nothing," Eli said. "I've cleaned up after you for the last time with the girls. You wouldn't find yourself constantly in hot water if you didn't insist on causing trouble. It's time for you to deal with this on your own." Eli put his hands up, showing he was done.

"Fine, if you don't care anymore, I can't make you!" She spun around and stormed back out the way she came. She got into her car, slammed the door, and peeled out of the parking lot.

Before the sound of Tandy's squealing departure died away, Thean came back in, his face still red with embarrassment.

"You're all set, Cassie." He handed her the keys.

"Thanks, I'll see you later, Thean." Unsettled, she walked out, keeping her gaze focused away from Eli and trying hard to get away before he said anything.

Her chest clenched, and her stomach churned. The bile rose in her throat. The tears blurred her vision, but she refused to give in. She lifted her chin and bit her lip to keep herself together.

. . .

THE FOLLOWING WEEKS, SHE IGNORED ELI'S CALLS. She deleted his voicemails without listening to them. Enaria and the girls from work kept her evenings busy. Confused and uncomfortable, she wasn't sure how she felt about him, or the idea of dating someone with such a volatile ex. It was a struggle not to reach out to him, but she had no history of dealing with that kind of drama. Her experience with past relationships had been boring and less entangled than his.

A month later, his persistence paid off when she answered her phone.

"Please, give me a chance to explain the scene at the shop."

Cassie hesitated, filled with uncertainty.

"Can we go to dinner? I want to explain Tandy's behavior."

A dozen excuses filled her mind. After a long pause, her resistance melted. There was just something about him. Not to mention the fantastic sex. It had been a while since the altercation in the garage, and maybe she had overreacted.

"Okay, Friday night. Six-thirty at the Old Steakhouse."

She hung up the phone, not convinced this was

the right decision. But she couldn't help herself. Thinking of him brought a smile to her face and made her stomach flutter.

CHAPTER 5

Clean-up On Aisle 5

Eli

Eli sat across from Cassie in a soft leather booth tucked in a corner of one of the best steakhouses in the city. When he met her in the lobby, their greeting was polite. Too polite. He needed all the help he could get to win another chance with her.

"Thank you for coming," he said.

"I almost didn't."

"But you're here." His voice was low, his fingers tightened on his glass.

Cassie nodded as she bit her bottom lip.

Eli watched her, waiting for her to say something, but she reached for her wine instead. As the ruby red liquid touched her lips, his pulse raced. He remembered the feel of her lips on his. He longed to kiss her again, to run his fingers through her hair. It had been a long time since he'd felt such stirrings. He'd thought his divorce had killed his sexual appetite until she walked into the shop that day and promptly took his breath away.

The server, a tall, super skinny, unnatural blonde, came to the table to take their order.

Cassie took another glance at the menu before setting it aside.

Eli ordered first, and she followed suit.

He cast another look around, noting the pendants hanging from the ceiling and the small candles on the table setting off dancing shadows in their wake. The atmosphere was quiet and relaxed.

"Now on to the uncomfortable topics," he said. "Talking about my ex-wife isn't my favorite pastime."

"I don't blame you," Cassie said. "She's sort of like a Tsunami."

"Sorry about that. Tandy's a lot to take in. It's worse when she's in one of her moods."

"It looked more like a raging storm."

He took a deep pull of his drink. "Believe me, that was one of her milder tantrums."

"Are you kidding?" Cassie sucked in an audible breath. "How do you handle it?"

"I try to keep things calm for the sake of the girls."

"Tell me about your daughters." She took a sip of her wine.

"I have one daughter, Addison. She's three."

"I'm confused. You said girls," Cassie said.

"I'm sorry. I know it's confusing. It's complicated. Savannah is five. Tandy and I had been dating for about three months when she discovered she was pregnant. I thought we should marry before the baby was born. A few months after Savannah was born, Tandy became pregnant with Addison. The girls are fourteen months apart."

Cassie's gaze locked with his as she wrapped her fingers around her wineglass.

"Being in our early twenties, we were too young, and having two kids back-to-back was stressful. How would I support them? I dropped out of the Engineering program at North Carolina State to work full time after we married. I had only worked at the shop part-time while in school."

The waitress stopped by their table. "Can I get you another round?"

He looked at his empty glass, surprised. "Yes, please."

Cassie nodded, and the waitress walked away.

Her hands clenched around her wineglass. Her shoulders tensed.

He was afraid to scare her away further with the details. But she deserved to know everything if they would have a chance.

"In what way?" she asked.

Their first course arrived. The waitress set the salad in front of Cassie, and the soup before him, before slipping away. The clam chowder burned his mouth on the first bite. It was hotter than he remembered from his last visit with Thean a few months ago.

"Because of my actions and going straight to the lawyer, I only provide support for Addison. So, she made up non-existent expenses like child care to supplement it."

"I don't understand?"

"There's a set amount calculated based on the number of children, custody terms, and incomes of both parents."

"Did she try to argue about Savannah?"

"The judge had a copy of the paternity tests right there in black and white."

"Ouch!" Cassie's jaw clenched.

The waitress came back to clear away the half-eaten dishes they'd set aside and to tell them their dinner would be ready in a few minutes.

"Her response was, since I didn't have to support Savannah, I shouldn't get visitation of her, and the judge agreed."

"That had to be heartbreaking."

"It blindsided me, to be honest. I hadn't considered that could happen. I wanted to kick myself for being stupid, standing there dumbstruck at the judge's decision. I was angry about all her manipulations. It never dawned on me she'd be a spiteful—so spiteful that she wouldn't allow me to see Savannah."

"I'm so sorry."

"I was the only father Savannah knew, and suddenly I was gone. She isn't allowed to come with me when I pick up Addison."

"Can't you talk to Tandy about it?"

"I've tried. But I can't get through to her. I swear the look she gave me in court that day was one of triumph. It was like she gloated. I won a single skirmish, but she'd won the whole damn battle, and relished the pain it caused me." He sipped his fresh drink.

"She wants you back," Cassie said. "I saw that much."

"She doesn't know what she wants. She's seeing her ex again, but I'm sure her parents don't know. They aren't fond of Luke."

"Why was she expecting you for dinner as a family?"

"That's one of the little games she plays. She likes to guilt me into coming over for dinner and spending the night because I drank too much wine."

"Does that happen often?"

Eli shook his head. "It's not what you think. It happened once. I slept in the girls' room and locked the door and left before she awoke."

Cassie frowned as she raised her wineglass.

I wish I knew what was going on in that mind of hers.

"I married her trying to do the right thing. I didn't realize how little I knew her, or her motivations, until after I left."

The waitress arrived with their dinner, and they picked at the food on their plates. His appetite was gone. A quick glance said hers was as well.

"Cassie, I know I have no right to ask this of

you, especially after a single date, but I would like to give this a chance if you're willing." He hoped he didn't sound as desperate as he felt.

She took a sip of wine, set it down, and took a deep breath before responding. "Same here, though I'm not sure how I feel about your ex. But I think I'd like to get to know you better, too."

This made him smile. He liked the vibes he was getting. He was glad they had talked tonight, and that she'd heard his side of the story.

Damn, I hope she doesn't run now.

CHAPTER 6

An Early Morning Call

Cassie

Cassie dialed the phone while her computer loaded. She shivered at the chill in the air and sipped her hot coffee. The office was eerily quiet.

Other than the large window overlooking the nice courtyard, her office was the typical corporate set up. Plain white walls and gray laminate office furniture. At least the chair was ergonomic and comfortable, and she was in an enclosed office. Not that the fishbowl set up she hated with a passion.

There was nothing worse than the open floor

plan some offices hosted that could turn any sane person into a germaphobe, as people clear across the room sneezed or coughed.

The phone connected, and her best friend from college answered.

"Good morning, this is Tamsen."

"Hey, girl. How are you this fine morning?"

"Cassie, it's so good to hear your voice. I'm fantastic. How's the job going?" Tamsen's voice sounded so clear, considering she was on her car phone. Almost as if she was in the office with her.

"Good, I think." Cassie scanned the view framed in her office window. The sun crept over the tops of the buildings across the way, casting crimson tinted shadows.

"What's on your mind?"

"I met someone. His name's Eli."

"Who is he?"

"Don't laugh. He's Morris' new mechanic."

"A grease monkey?" Tamsen paused. "Okay."

"I know. Not my usual type."

"Spill." Tamsen's hearty laugh pierced through the quiet office.

"He runs the shop where I've been taking Morris. He's a longtime friend of Finn's."

"Have you gone out with him yet?"

"Once."

"Ok—ay… What am I missing?" Tamsen asked.

Traffic blared in the background. Car horns bleated like an orchestral choir tuning up before a performance. It was a familiar morning occurrence in Manhattan where Tamsen lived and worked.

"He's divorced with two little girls."

Tamsen sighed. "That's a Pandora's box best left unopened."

Cassie sucked in a breath.

"But you opened it. Didn't you?" Cassie's hands gripped the phone a little tighter.

"And I still wonder what the hell I was thinking."

Tamsen was the reason Cassie wanted to give Eli another chance. "You and Drew are perfect together."

"Yet his ex-wife has haunted us every step of the way," Tamsen grumbled.

"That's what I'm afraid of," Cassie confided. "I got a glimmer of her, and it scared the shit out of me."

"See what I mean?"

"There has to be normal ex-wives out there." Cassie swiped at the hair that was tickling her nose.

"A few do exist," Tamsen conceded.

"I need to believe that. You should have seen the whirlwind that followed this woman into Eli's shop. She'd have made Cruella de Vil proud."

"Wow," Tamsen said.

"I wish more divorces were civil."

"I do, too. I keep hoping one day Ingrid will stop being so nasty and let Dax visit again."

"It's got to be hard for Drew."

"We miss him. But with Drew traveling so much, it's best for right now."

Cassie twisted the phone cord around her finger while pressing the receiver against her ear, lost in thought.

"You there?" Tamsen asked.

"Hmm. Yes. Sorry."

"Spacing out again, are you?"

"You know me too well." Cassie laughed, draining the last of her coffee with a sigh. "When will you be here again?"

"At the end of the month."

"It will be good to see you–" A car horn blasted in the background.

"That was close," Tamsen huffed out a breath.

"You okay?"

"Yeah, a cab almost hit a bike messenger."

"Ouch, that would have been a crappy way to start the morning."

"Yeah. Maybe while I'm there, I can meet your new guy?"

"Sure."

"I'd better let you go. I'm almost at the office."

"And I'm out of coffee. Give my love to Drew. I'll talk to you soon." Cassie put the phone back on the cradle and rose from her chair.

If Eli's ex was anything like Drew's ex-wife Ingrid, she wasn't sure she was up for the challenge. Images of Eli's ex screeching at him had an involuntary shudder coursing through her.

Shit. I might actually be in over my head.

She was nervous about meeting Eli for dinner. Her stomach did another flop. It had been doing that since she'd gotten off the phone with him. She didn't mention that part to Tamsen because she would have taken it as an omen to cancel.

It's too late now.

She'd agreed to go, and she'd meet him tonight to hear him out. Shaking her head out of her reverie, she stretched and grabbed her coffee cup before heading out of her office to the break room.

Cassie loved how Eli wanted to introduce her to new things. For their third date, he took her to a popular indoor rock wall. It was a brief and painful visit and never repeated. She was nowhere near as athletic or muscular as him. It was painfully clear as she dangled from the wall, unable to continue her ascent.

On the way out, she turned to him and grinned. "I don't think rock climbing is my thing."

Chuckling, he said, "I have to agree." He kissed the tip of her nose and took her hand in his.

Cassie and Eli became almost inseparable outside of work, meeting for dinner a few nights a week. The weekends Eli didn't have visits with his daughter, he went out with her.

It was always an adventure. They watched plays, visited local museums and art exhibits, went to dinner, and saw movies often.

They had been dating for a couple of months when she stopped by his shop on a weekday to meet for a quick lunch at Jenny's diner. In the car, heading back to the shop afterward, he lowered the convertible top, and fragrances of autumn lingered in the breeze. Bright rusts and reds of fallen leaves scattered around them, creating a beautiful post-card. Cassie bundled her hair in a messy bun so it wouldn't tangle in the wind, and Eli wore a baseball cap.

"How about dinner and a movie on Saturday?" he asked.

"I thought you had your daughter this weekend?"

"Addison's sick. Tandy is keeping her home. She hasn't been to school for the last three days. She must be pretty ill."

"I'm sorry to hear that she's ill again. I'd love to get together, though."

She seems sick and out of school often.

"Great, I look forward to it," he said.

She smiled at him as she took a deep breath, inhaling the sweet smells in the air.

"The car is handling funny." Eli glanced at her. "Was the steering loose for you?" This was the first time he'd driven her car in weeks.

"I haven't noticed anything."

"Strange. Thean aligned it and rotated the tires last month."

"I put air in the tires yesterday," she said. "One of the rear tires was low. I topped them all off."

"Topped them off? What do you mean?" His brow rose.

"You know, filled them up."

He sucked in an exaggerated breath, giving her the impression he was not happy.

"How much air did you add?"

"I'm not sure. Until they were full."

"How could you tell?"

"When the air stopped making noise, I guess." She shrugged.

"Tell me you're joking," he said, the surprise in his voice clear as he pulled in front of the shop.

"Why would I joke about that?"

"Cassie, did you measure the air?"

"No, why would I?" she asked, baffled by his question.

"Oh, Lord help me." He stole a quick glance at the sky. "To put in the right amount."

"How are you supposed to do that?"

"Here, I'll show you." He pulled the car in front of the big roll-up door to the garage and got out.

"Hey, Thean, bring me a tire gauge," he hollered.

Cassie wrung her hands as she stepped away from the car. She'd made some sort of guy faux pax... though she had no idea what.

"The label for the tire's PSI is on the side of the tire." He reached down to the tire wall and ran his hand over the raised numbers on the side of the tire. He pointed out what each meant.

"Oh," she said, her cheeks burning.

Thean walked out with the tire gauge and handed it over to Eli. "How are you, Cassie?"

"I'm in trouble."

"Ms. Cassie here fills up her tires without a gauge. Apparently, she fills them 'until they are full.'" He looked over at Thean and grinned.

Thean chuckled.

"Okay, let's see what we have here. These tires call for twenty-six pounds." His expression was serious as he kneeled to read the right front tire. "Thirty-five PSI," he said over his shoulder.

Thean stood next to Cassie, both off to the side as they watched Eli in action. Air hissed as Eli let it out of the tire.

He moved to the right rear tire. "Forty-three PSI in this one. Christ, this isn't good," he said, not looking up from the gauge.

She detected a note of frustration in his voice. Thean stayed quiet, though a strange look spread across his face as he ran his fingers through his tousled blonde hair. More air hissed.

Still not looking at her, Eli stood and walked to the left rear tire before he knelt again.

"Sixty!" He shook his head. The air was full of hissing now. He rose and walked to the front of the car. He glanced over at Thean again and shook his head.

Cassie couldn't read his face well enough to know how upset he was. She was uncomfortable with the focus on her.

"Well, I'll be damned. I didn't see this one coming. Thean, she's certifiable," he said, as he stood up next to the car. "Ninety freaking PSI!"

Thean looked over at her, eyes wide. "Holy crap, Cassie! You're lucky you didn't have a blowout. You could've been killed!"

"I didn't realize. I'm sorry." She cringed as heat filled her face.

"Seriously, what am I going to do with you?" Eli broke straight for her. Stuffing the gauge in his back pocket, he reached for her, wrapping his arms around her.

"I guess you'll just have to maintain my car," she said.

"I think that's safer for everyone," he agreed as he kissed her.

Thean bobbed his head vigorously.

Cassie grimaced and nodded before she returned Eli's kiss.

Why not? It works for me.

CHAPTER 7

Moving On

Cassie

Cassie sat across from Eli in the booth at the end of the row by the window. Jenny's Diner was quiet today. It was early still, with none of the usual bustle of people filling the place for the lunch rush yet. She fiddled with the straw in her iced tea as she listened to him.

"What do you think about moving in together?" he asked.

Her breath caught in her throat. *Shit. Things were moving fast.*

Eli focused on his lunch. A Pastrami Rueben on

lightly toasted marbled rye, dripping with extra sauce, and the same sides always came with it potato salad made fresh daily and a crisp dill pickle.

She had never seen him order anything else. "Is it because you think I need to spend more time with your daughter?" She picked at her roast beef sandwich. Her stomach was in knots now.

"Yes," he said. "We're together almost every night and every other weekend. I don't see why we shouldn't live together instead of going back and forth between our places."

"Don't you think that would push things with your ex?" Though they had been dating a few months, she wasn't sure she was ready for another episode of '*Tandyvision*'. She couldn't repeat that last scene.

"You'll have to get to know Addison if we continue."

"Your ex scares the hell out of me."

"Honestly, Tandy's all bark."

"I'm sure that's what they said about Cujo too, and look how that turned out." She took a bite of her sandwich to avoid saying more.

"With Hank moving out, the timing makes sense, and this way you won't need a new roommate. Give it a chance, please? I hate going home alone. I love the time we spend together, and I know you do, too."

"Okay, let's give it a try." She wanted Eli in her life, and she knew she would have to build a relationship with his daughter. He was right. She couldn't keep things separate forever. She bit her lip. All she could do was go with it and hope it wouldn't blow up in her face.

TWO WEEKS LATER, ELI EMPTIED HIS SMALL STORAGE unit into her place. Her second-floor apartment was a small two bed and one bath. She grinned at Eli on his way up the stairs with an armful of clothes. Watching him brought lustful memories of their first night together.

They rearranged things to make it homier. After all the changes, the apartment had shrunk. At least that's how it felt. She decorated Addison's space with butterflies stenciled on the newly painted, pale peach, and sea-foam green colored walls. Addison had made a comment once during lunch they had a few months prior, and Cassie had taken her interests to heart.

"It's going to be an adjustment, but you'll see,

it'll be fine." He wrapped his arms around her shoulders.

"I hope Addison doesn't mind the desk set up in her room."

"She'll only care that the computer plays movies, I promise."

"I suppose it'll work since she'll only be here part time."

Eli had told her he was confident it would all fall into place in time. She hoped he was right.

A month later, she wondered why Addison still hadn't been over for a visit.

———

Cassie was sitting on the couch, the evening news on the television, when Eli stormed into the apartment, slamming the door behind him.

"I'm going fishing." He tossed his keys in the ceramic bowl on the side table, making the bowl slide a few inches.

"What happened?"

"Tandy called, and as usual, she pissed me off."

Getting up from the couch, she followed him into the bedroom and stood by the door while he rummaged around in the closet.

He pulled a small duffle bag from under the bed and stuffed clothes into it. He walked past her and out of the room, his unzipped bag overflowing with clothes.

"She married Luke yesterday. Apparently, Addison and Savannah are so happy Luke is Addison's new daddy." He paused in the hall and turned to her. "She had the nerve to tell me that since I walked out, the girls needed a father and Luke was stepping up."

"Oh, Eli, I'm sorry. She's just trying to get under your skin."

"She put Addison on the phone and had her tell me about her new daddy, Luke."

Cassie cringed at the image it invoked in her head. *What a spiteful woman!*

"Yeah, *I'm* the bad guy because *she* lied and slept around. But I should have stayed, anyway."

Cassie considered saying something comforting, but Eli wasn't in a listening mood.

"With Luke back in town, and learning Savannah is his, he's all about being a standup guy now," Eli continued. His fingers motioned air quotes.

"You're still Addison's father, and she knows that. Maybe there will be less drama if Tandy is happy," Cassie said, trying to soothe his temper.

"She taunted me, made insinuations about you, said things like I've moved on, and she needed to do the same."

"At least she's moving on. Focus on that."

"It's been a long week. I need to get away," he said, sounding calmer.

"Want company?"

He snorted. "It's not your kind of place." He gave a snarky laugh and slung a pair of socks into his duffle bag.

"What's that supposed to mean?"

"I'll be roughing it."

"Excuse me?" she asked again.

"You can't take your blow dryer," he said. He walked out to the patio to grab his fishing rods.

"Did you hear me ask if I could?"

"Seriously, the cabin is rustic. No electricity. No indoor plumbing. It's just a simple two-room log cabin by a lake. The outhouse is around back."

"That sounds rustic, all right." The outhouse was almost a deal-breaker, but she would manage it. "Well, if you can handle it, so can I."

"All right." He didn't sound convinced. "But it'll be cold, so make sure you pack thermals." He tossed his duffel bag over his shoulder as he hauled the gear downstairs.

She figured it would be a bonding moment for them if she survived. She wasn't a roughing it kind of girl, but she would try something outside her comfort zone for him.

Eli packed the sleeping bags while she grabbed extra blankets and plenty of warm clothes, just in case. If this was such a rustic place, she would need them.

They bought basic provisions at the grocery store on the edge of town. When they got to the cabin, he took in the groceries.

"If you could unpack, I'll look around to make sure everything is sound and then I'll build us a fire," he said.

"Sounds good," she said.

The cabin appeared solid and well-insulated from the elements. She took it all in as she walked through the front door into the modest family room. She couldn't wait to light the large wood-burning fireplace that had a homey quality about it. The wood floors were unvarnished but smooth.

The windows were small and dirty, but were clear enough to see through and let in light. She rolled her eyes at the set of antlers on the wall. The one touch of class was a painting of a bighorn sheep climbing the jagged peaks.

An old 1970s style paisley couch sat in the center of the room facing the fireplace. It looked clean. The little kitchenette had a tiny counter and a camp stove set on it, a box of matchsticks beside it.

She tossed the bags on the bed in the single bedroom off to the side of the main room and then went into the kitchen to boil water. It took a few attempts to get the stove started. When she finally got it lit, she grinned at her accomplishment.

When Eli walked in a few minutes later, she handed him a tall steaming mug.

"What's this?"

"Hot cocoa," she said.

He took a sip. "Hmm. Perfect. Thank you." He closed his eyes and licked the foam from his lips.

They crawled into bed just after sunset, skipping dinner, exhausted from the long drive. Eli was still tense and distant, so she didn't push him. He would open up when he was ready.

The next morning, Cassie found herself alone when the sun came up. A note said he'd gone fishing at the lake. Curled up on the worn couch with a cup of tea, she spent her morning reading paperbacks and enjoying the peaceful environment. She'd have preferred a few more amenities, but overall, she managed well enough.

After a simple dinner, they sat on the floor, the small coffee table between them, and Eli slaughtered her at chess.

"I give up," she laughed.

"Let's sit outside on the porch and watch the stars."

"I love it. Let me make tea first."

Twenty minutes later, she joined him on the porch with two steaming mugs. Spearmint, lavender, and chamomile filled her nose. They snuggled on the large wooden swing, and Eli wrapped a warm fleece blanket over their shoulders. They sipped tea, and he pointed out constellations he knew as the stars sparkled in the clear night sky. An hour later, Cassie shivered as the fog rolled in.

"Let's get you into bed," Eli suggested.

Her teeth chattered. She nodded, unable to speak. She carried the empty mugs into the kitchen while Eli added another blanket over the bed.

He was already under the covers when she came in. Stripping, she dropped her clothes where she stood, pulled on her sweats and sweatshirt, and jumped in beside him. Scooting closer, she laid her head on his chest and nestled into his embrace. His skin was hot, and the warmth filled her.

He ran his fingers through her hair. The gentle caresses soothed her. Her eyes drifted closed.

"I'm so glad you came. I should have given you more credit. You never struck me as the roughing it in the woods kind of woman."

Cassie smiled against his chest. "I'm not, but you needed a break, and I wanted to be there for you."

"I love you."

"Love you too," she whispered. Slumber took her quickly.

By the time they left the cabin, the tension had been shed, and both were more relaxed than they had been in weeks.

CHAPTER 8

Mommy Hates You

Cassie

Cassie's nerves were strung tight. It had been a few weeks since their camping trip, and tonight was Addison's first visit to the apartment. She needed the weekend to go well.

Shortly before dinner, Eli came in with Addison in his arms. She had her face tucked into his neck, her pigtails bounced as they walked.

"Addison, this is Cassie. Can you say hello?"

Bright chocolate eyes turned to her, and she smiled. "Hi."

"Hello Addison, are you hungry?"

The little girl nodded.

"Great, we have chicken and mac and cheese for you. How does that sound?"

"Good," Addison said.

Eli took her into the bathroom and washed her up, then set her at the table.

Addison was the spitting image of her mother, though Addison's nature was far more agreeable.

Cassie was sorry she hadn't gotten to know Eli's daughter better before. On her way to bed, Cassie paused as Eli's voice filtered from Addison's bedroom. She stood rooted in the hall just outside the doorway at Addison's soft voice.

"Daddy, why does Mommy hate you?"

The words stunned Cassie. He would have to tread water with this one, but she hoped he would be honest at the same time. A half-truth now would just come back later to bite them.

"Honey, what makes you think your mom hates me?" Eli asked.

"Oh, Daddy," Addison said in a huff and sighed as only a three-and-a-half-year-old could pull off.

Cassie couldn't see them through the crack, their hushed voices barely above a whisper from her spot on the other side of the door.

"Mommy always says mean things about you."

"I'm sorry. Mommy and Daddy have some things we need to work out. The only thing you need to remember is that no matter what, I love you."

"Mommy said Cassie is why you don't love us anymore."

"Addy, that's not true. I love you and Savannah. That will never change. Your mom and I divorced long before I met Cassie."

"If you still love Savannah, why can't she visit you? Is it because Cassie doesn't want her to?"

"Honey, that couldn't be further from the truth. Cassie has been so eager to meet you. She made this room just for you. She wants you to be happy and for this to feel like home. Of course, she wants you here."

Cassie remained in the hall, her back pressed against the wall, desperate to be a part of this conversation. But Addison wouldn't be so honest with Eli if she were in the room. Cassie was a bystander in this relationship.

"As for Savannah, sweetheart, I'd love to see her. She's welcome to visit anytime she'd like to, but it doesn't work that way."

Cassie's heart broke, and she clasped her hands

over her mouth to keep from making a sound. Her eyes teared up as she listened to this little girl repeat the distorted impressions she had of him. It was clear Tandy had no boundaries about attacking him.

"Why not?"

"I'm not Savannah's daddy."

"Why does that matter if you love her?"

"It matters because the judge said so. When your mom and I divorced, he gave me visitation with you because I am your daddy. But I couldn't get the same visitation for Savannah. Believe me, I tried. Your mother just won't let me see her."

"Can't you ask the judge to change his mind?" Addison's little voice pleaded.

"I'm sorry, honey, but it doesn't work that way. Savannah gets to spend those weekends with her daddy."

"But she wants to see *you*."

Eli cleared his throat, and it sounded as if he was choking on his own misery. "You tell Savannah that I love her, and she's welcome here anytime. Now it's getting late. You should have been asleep an hour ago."

Cassie peeked into the room just as Eli kissed Addison and switched off her bedside lamp. It left the room dark except for the soothing light coming from the stuffed turtle tucked into her arms. Gentle sounds of the ocean filled the room to lull her to sleep. This was her favorite toy, and apparently, she refused to sleep without it. Cassie stepped away from the opening just as Eli stood up from the bedside. As he reached the door, Addison called out to him.

"Daddy, can Seshat sleep with me?"

"I'll leave the door cracked, and if she wants to come in, she can."

"Okay…" Addison sounded like she wanted to argue the point, but then said, "I love you, Daddy."

"Goodnight sweetheart, I love you too."

He quietly backed out of the room, stumbling into her as he turned towards their room. He put his finger to his lips.

When they reached their room, she moved to sit on the chaise lounge at the foot of their bed. Unsure what to say, she bit back her anger and frustration, chewing on the inside of her cheek. She wanted to comfort him, but didn't know how.

He came over and sat down beside her. After a long, quiet moment, he rubbed his eyes and let out a breath, reaching for her hand. "I wish you didn't have to hear things like that," he said, his voice almost inaudible.

"That woman is toxic. How dare she make the girls feel this way? You warned me she was bitter, but this was a surprise. You need to fix the impression Tandy's given her, though. It's not right that Savannah thinks you don't love her, or that she isn't good enough to see you. It's not right that Addison believes it, either. What Tandy's doing is wrong!" Her voice rising with indignation, the words escaping before she could stifle them. She took a breath to steady herself.

"I'm not shocked Tandy's bashing me to the girls. But it hurt like hell to hear it from Addison tonight." With his shoulders hunched and fists clenched, he dropped his hands to his lap.

She leaned into him and rested against his shoulder.

The anger left him as he pulled her closer and pressed his cheek on her head. "I love you. I know I don't tell you often enough, but I'm so glad you're here."

They sat with their arms wrapped around each other. She had never seen him like this. He seemed so defeated. He stared at a picture of Savannah and Addison on the bureau while she stroked his cheek.

She was worried about the effect Tandy's cruelty had on him. It was hard to hear those words from one's daughter.

Cassie had a fitful night instead of a restful slumber. The fairytales of her childhood were now haunting her.

She was in the middle of a Disney Princess story. Not as the beautiful princess who found her true love and lived happily ever after. Instead, she was cast in the role of the Evil Queen or the Wicked Stepmother, with Tandy portrayed as Snow White.

She tossed and turned, dreaming of Addison's bedtime conversation with Eli, crossing paths with her childhood. She pictured herself in Addison's place. Cassie's childhood had not been traumatic, though often isolated and alone. She had grown up being treated like an unplanned burden by her parents.

Her dreams twisted again, bringing a new perspective. In both Cinderella and Snow White, the stepmothers were presented as horrible, evil, selfish people treating their stepdaughters cruelly. Their mothers and fathers were not alive, and one couldn't get a poor impression of them, so it was all about the wicked stepmothers. The dreams bombarded her with images of herself as evil and cruel, with Addison cowering away from her.

With another shift, the movie in her head changed to Ever After, and she found herself in Anjelica Huston's role of the new wife. A woman who, from the beginning, was reminded she married someone whose first love was someone other than her.

It was a painful insight into her new role. The constant, unmistakable feeling she didn't matter. Once again, traveling back into her childhood role of not being wanted or needed, and the prevailing attitude that since she was there, they might as well deal with her.

Except that in Eli's case, he only married Tandy while trying to do the right thing.

The next morning, she woke exhausted and disillusioned. She hoped this state wouldn't last long because she wasn't sure she could handle it.

More Scheming

Eli

wo weeks later, Eli walked up the long flagstone path to the front door. He reached for the bell and then halted as voices floated from around back. He strolled around the expansive house to the backyard of his ex-in-laws' house. Tandy would be out of town this week-end, so he agreed to pick up Addison to make it easier for her. A calm breeze tossed around the smells of freshly cut grass and blooming roses. Today's mild temperatures meant the girls would play in the backyard while his ex-mother-in-law,

Corrine, drank a mint julep on the sprawling back patio. The flowerbeds and lawn were in a pristine condition as usual–everything perfect and in its place.

Now by the edge of the house, he saw the girls on the lawn playing together and heard the unexpected voice of his ex. His ex-mother-in-law was lecturing Tandy.

Eli paused for a moment to watch the girls together. God, how he missed seeing Savannah. He hesitated at the corner, not wanting to get caught eavesdropping, but his curiosity eventually won.

Tandy stood, rooted a few feet away, on the patio with her mother.

Listening to Tandy's mother berate her was not a pleasant experience.

"I can't believe you let him get away," Corrine said.

"The divorce is final. He's not coming back."

"I can't believe you chose Luke over Eli. I'll never understand. Of all the men to be involved with, why Luke? I thought I'd raised you better than that, to be a proper southern wife."

"I know, Mama."

"Well?"

"Eli's seeing someone else now and he'll never

forgive me for Savannah." In a hushed whisper, she said, "and I'm married to Luke."

"You should have figured out a way to get rid of her?"

"Eli will never forgive me for Savannah."

"Well, if you hadn't let Luke back in, none of this would have happened. Eli would never have known about Savannah." Her mother continued.

"I screwed up." Tandy hung her head.

Son-of-a-bitch. Corrine knew. He should have known. Torn between pity and an urge to strangle her, Eli almost felt sorry for Tandy as she squirmed before her mother.

"Yes, you did. You made a mess of things, not just for you this time. Those girls need a better man in their lives than Luke."

Tandy sat at the table across from her mother and poured a drink from the tall glass pitcher sitting in the center of the table.

Frustration pulsed through him as Tandy endured her mother's verbal lashings. Tandy had chosen Luke long before their divorce, and her mother knew it. *The witch.* Just thinking about it made him angry all over again.

"Tandy, are you listening?"

"Yes, Mama."

"What will you do?"

"I'll think of something, Mama."

Eli shook his head. This was why she was so screwed up, because she let her mother ride roughshod over her. Teaching her to use and abuse men, and when that didn't work, to bring in the big artillery, the girls. Who knew what her next scheme to please her mother would be?

Eli drew in a deep breath. Sometimes, there were things you wished you had never learned. But it didn't matter. The divorce was final, and he was not going back.

Savannah came around the corner, and spotting him, threw herself into his arms. "Daddy!" she squealed in delight.

"Hey pumpkin, how are you doing?" He hugged her close as his chest tightened and his stomach dropped. He met Tandy's gaze over her head.

Tandy was quick to turn her eyes away and exchange a conspiratorial look with her mother.

"Hello, Eli," Tandy said.

"Hi." He gave a brisk nod.

"Thanks for coming by to pick up Addison. It's much easier on me." Tandy rubbed her swollen hands over her slightly protruding belly.

"Is she ready to go?"

"Yes, she is," Tandy said.

"Let me fix you a drink," Corrine said.

"I have to get back on the road."

"Can I come with you this time?" Savannah mumbled, standing next to him, still holding his hand.

Eli looked up at Tandy and her mother, hoping this time would be different, but at their lack of response, he looked back at Savannah. "I wish honey, but your grand-momma has big plans for you this weekend."

"But I want to go with you and Addy. I never get to go with you," she cried.

"I know, baby." He glared at Tandy.

"Savannah, come here," Tandy commanded.

He leaned down to give Savannah a hug and whispered, "I love you," in her ear. He tenderly kissed the top of her head and said goodbye. As he looked up, he caught his ex-mother-in-law watching him. Her face was passive. She gave nothing away. He fought to keep his composure. Addison didn't need to see him lose it.

Savannah shuffled back to her mother, still pleading with her, while Addison ambled over, holding her stuffed turtle and a blanket.

"You ready?" Eli asked. His voice was thick as he choked out the words.

Addison nodded, and they walked away, hand in hand.

They had barely rounded the corner of the house when he heard Tandy's mother berating her again. His gut clenched.

"You need to stop punishing him with Savannah. You should let him take both girls together."

"If he gave a damn about Savannah, he wouldn't have left us."

"Maybe if you did, the two of you could work things out from there. My point is, if you were nicer to him, you'd get him back…"

Focused on getting Addison buckled in. He didn't hear Tandy's response and didn't care to. Savannah's tear-streaked face and little pleading voice broke his heart because he was to blame for the end result. He loved Savannah. His gut reaction —leaving Tandy the way he had—made this mess, and he couldn't take it back.

He drove away while Addison sat quietly and stared out the side window. He was grateful she couldn't see his tears.

Cassie was excited that Eli turned the weekend with Addison into an adventure. Their first trip to the Children's Discovery Museum was fantastic. The more time they spent together, the more comfortable she was with her growing relationship with him and his daughter. Addison was a joy to have, full of energy and excitement. Eli had been reserved since he came home with Addison, but when asked, he shook his head and said they would talk about it later. Cassie left it alone, choosing to focus on having fun with Addison instead.

Addison reached for her hand and dragged her over to one of the open exhibits. She showed her how the static ball worked. Eli stood back, watching with a smile on his lips. Addison giggled as sparks and spots under their fingertips crackled. When Addison pulled her hands off the glass ball, she took one of Cassie's hands again. Cassie smiled and reached over to pat her head and tuck her hair behind her ears. It was such a great day. She wished it didn't have to end.

That night, after tucking Addison in, Eli wrapped his arm around Cassie and led her from the room. At the door, just as Cassie reached out to flick the light switch, Addison peeked her head out of the covers.

"Cassie?"

"Yes, love?"

"I had fun with you today." The pile of blankets near her face muffled Addison's voice.

"I had fun with you today too, sweetheart. Sweet dreams."

"You too. G'night daddy."

"Night, baby. See you in the morning."

Eli kissed the top of Cassie's head as she flipped the switch. They glided from the room in each other's arms, leaving the bedroom door open behind them.

It felt as though she had made a breakthrough with Addison, and her spirits were high. Surely, this was a good portent for the future.

CHAPTER 10

An Allegation of Abuse

Cassie

Cassie and Eli had been living together for a few months, and things had been going well. The weather was cooler than usual for the first week of August. The three of them went to the Carolina Raptor Center inside the Latta Plantation Nature Preserve during an overnight visit with Addison. By the time they got moving and in the car, it was mid-morning.

"I better call Tandy and tell her we might be late tonight. I don't want to wait and give her the chance to ruin our day while we're there," Eli said.

"That's a safe bet," Cassie agreed.

He grabbed his cell phone from the center console. Tandy answered on the third ring.

"Hi, Tandy."

"Eli."

"We got a late start. I'm calling because I might be a little late meeting up with you this evening. I can bring Addison directly to you to make it easier. We're headed to the Raptor Center—"

"You have no right to go there. That's something we should do as a family!" she shrieked.

He looked over as Cassie cringed at Tandy's screams through the phone.

"Tandy, we aren't a family anymore. You can take the girls with Luke."

Tandy hung up the phone. He shrugged.

"You okay?" Cassie asked as she reached to pat his hand.

"Yeah." He stole a quick glance in the rear-view mirror again. "Thank God, Addy's asleep." They were close to the park, and he would have to wake her soon.

The exhibitions fascinated Addison. Her curiosity and boundless energy were contagious, and the day flew by.

"Can we see the birds again?" Addison asked.

"You've seen them three times already." He laughed.

"I know, but they're pretty."

"Let's go, at least. It's cooler inside," Cassie said. As Addison reached for her, the three of them held hands as they walked through the darkened maze of birds.

"That was fun. Can we go to the bird hospital now?"

"Sure."

They walked over to the hospital wing and waited for the tour to start. Eli had Addison giggling as he tickled her to keep her occupied while they waited. They saw as many exhibits as possible before Addison lost her steam.

It wasn't until late afternoon that an exhausted Addison was ready to go home.

"I need to go potty," she said.

"Okay, honey."

The bathrooms were across from the exit of the bird hospital.

"I can take her into the women's restroom. That way, you won't have to take her into the men's," Cassie offered.

"That would be great. Thanks. Is that okay with you, Addy?"

Addison nodded. Cassie smiled as she tucked Addison's small hand in her palm and led the way to the women's restroom. After they finished, they joined him under the large magnolia outside the door.

Worn out from their much-enjoyed day, they left the park. In the car, on the way home, Eli called Tandy as Addison fell asleep in the back seat.

"Yeah," Tandy snapped.

"We've left the park. I'll drop Addison off."

"No. I'll pick Addison up. I don't want to wait that long." The growl in Tandy's voice told him she was spoiling for a fight.

"Okay, we'll be home by six."

"Fine."

When they arrived, Tandy was nowhere to be seen. Eli woke Addison and led her upstairs. Cassie walked up behind him.

"I'll run to the store real quick. We're out of coffee creamer," Cassie said, shutting the refrigerator door.

"Ah, the sacred ingredient to your morning coffee," Eli laughed. "Or are you skipping out to avoid Tandy?"

"You know me too well." Cassie shrugged.

A quick kiss on the cheek, a wave goodbye to Addison, and out the door, she went.

Cassie picked up a few non-essentials just to drag out time and avoid the wrath of Eli's ex before heading home. She still remembered the last time she was in the same room as Tandy.

"How did it go?" she asked as she came in the door.

"Fine. She didn't say a word. She grabbed Addison's bag and left." Eli wrapped his arms around her and kissed her deeply.

"What was her deal?"

"Who knows with her?"

"Oh well, it was a nice day. The Eagle Nesting program was precious."

"It was. The little birds fascinated Addy. It's good to see her bond with you."

Cassie kissed him. "You sound as though you had doubts." She tightened her arms around him.

"Not doubts, just concerns. The divorce has been hard on her."

"I think she's adjusting well." She kissed him

again and then turned on the oven. She reached for a bottle of wine. "I grabbed a pre-made lasagna, and a new Merlot I thought we'd try. I'm exhausted."

He took the bottle from her and opened it. "A quick, quiet dinner sounds great. Thanks." He poured two glasses and handed one to her.

Forty-five minutes later, they sat down and ate, and then after dinner, they went to bed early, snuggled up in each other's arms. The perfect ending to an almost perfect day.

HANDS FULL, SHE GRAPPLED TO OPEN THE DOOR, juggling a bag of groceries on one arm, her purse, and keys on the other. It had been another long day at work and Cassie was grateful it was over.

The phone rang just as she got through the door. She dumped her purse on the couch, and the bag of groceries on the kitchen counter, next to her pile of keys, and grabbed the receiver.

"You're finally home." Enaria sounded harried.

"I just walked in."

"I don't think we're ready for tomorrow's meeting." The diatribe was undaunted by the lack of participation on Cassie's part.

Cassie was exhausted. Her head spun from a headache brewing. "We'll be fine, Enaria, we've got it. All we have to do is tidy the presentation for the meeting."

"I hate it when the muckity mucks show up to check on us peons. Why are they coming from New York, anyway?"

"To mess with your head."

"Funny."

"I try. Don't stress. The work is done. I'll finish it in the morning. We'll be fine," Cassie said.

Turning towards the refrigerator, she noticed a note propped against the coffee maker. Eli always left her notes to say *hi*, or he'd be late. With her empty hand, she laid the note flat and read it.

"If you say so, I'll be in early to help since I get to drop the girls off at band practice on the way in…" Her mind went blank. "Hmm."

"What's wrong?" Enaria said.

She stood still for a full minute, a bag of apples in her hands as she re-read the note Eli had left.

What the hell.

"Cassie, is everything ok?" She heard the concern in Enaria's voice.

"Eli left me a weird note." The pain in her head grew stronger.

"Is he going to be late?"

"It doesn't say."

"Well, what does it say?" Enaria's voice now impatient.

Cassie wasn't thinking clearly. The headache was racing towards a full-blown migraine, her stomach roiling.

"It says, '*Tandy called. Addison was sexually abused. The doctor confirmed it.*'" She dropped the bag of apples on the counter as the words penetrated through the fog.

"He left that in a note? Who does that?" Shock resonated in her friend's voice.

She gripped the edge of the counter as her knees grew weak.

"There are no other details. I need to call him."

"Oh, honey. Call him and find out what's going on. If there's anything you need, please call!"

"Yeah. I need to go." Her head was throbbing now. Swallowing back the bile as nausea kicked in, she called his cell, but it went directly to voicemail.

"Hey babe, it's me. Got your note. I'm worried. Please call me and let me know you and Addison are okay. I love you." She kept her tone light. He didn't need to know she was freaking out. She hung up, staring at the phone as if it would give her an answer.

Hands shaking, she put away the groceries. She kept staring at the phone, willing it to ring. Her migraine reached a new level. There were now spots dancing in her vision. Struggling to keep her mind occupied, she stepped into the shower and washed her hair. She'd have to wait until Eli came home to understand what was going on.

After a hot, soothing shower, she popped a couple of over-the-counter migraine pills and settled on the couch with a cup of tea and flipped on the television. Seshat hopped up to the armrest, gently head-butting Cassie's arm, making tea slosh around. Cassie switched the cup to her other hand, stroking the cat's head.

She couldn't concentrate on the TV. Finishing her tea, she walked into the kitchen and put her cup in the sink. Looking at the phone, she wished he would respond. Giving in to her need to reach him, she called again. Once more, it went straight to voicemail.

After a quick, "Honey, call me, please," she hung up, curled up on the couch. Picking up Seshat, she absently rubbed the cat's ears.

The phone rang, startling her as she flinched and Seshat jumped off the couch.

Eli was calling her back.

"What did Eli say? What's going on?" Enaria asked, as she put the phone to her ear.

Cassie slumped against the counter.

Not Eli. Damn it.

"I don't know. He hasn't called yet."

"What the hell?"

"I wish I knew. I feel incredibly helpless right now." Her voice broke.

"I'll let you go. Please call me when you find out."

She nodded.

"Cassie?"

Shaking her head, obviously Enaria couldn't see her. "Okay. Bye."

The veins in her head continued to pulse and throb as she made her way back to the couch.

Eli didn't come home, and he never called her back.

The next morning, Cassie woke on the couch after a restless sleep.

Rushing through the morning ritual, she didn't have time to call Eli until she'd made it to the office. Again, the call went to voicemail. She tried not to panic, but the continued silence was scaring the hell out of her. As she was setting the phone back in the cradle, Enaria stuck her head in.

"Morning," Enaria said.

"Hey."

"Is everything okay? What did Eli say?"

"He didn't come home." Her eyes welled. She pressed her knuckles against them to stop the flow.

"Oh… But you talked to him, right?"

Cassie shook her head. "I left two voicemails before I fell asleep on the couch. He never called back. He's still not answering either. I have no idea if Addison is okay."

"Why leave that in a note, though?"

"I don't know." Her hands shook again. She had to tuck them under her legs to make it stop. "I hate sitting here doing nothing. Not knowing what's happening."

"I can't imagine."

"Poor Addy, she must be freaking out!" Cassie's lip trembled as she looked down at her desk. Then she jumped to her feet. "I can't do this right now. Let's get this presentation together before I lose my mind."

Enaria firmed her shoulders and sat on the edge of Cassie's desk. "If you're sure you're up to it!"

They worked non-stop for the next two hours, though Cassie took frequent glances at the phone on her desk. She was often sidetracked, but she redirected her focus to the presentation. It had to be flawless.

The morning flew by with the stress of the meeting preparations, and she didn't have time to call Eli until lunchtime. This time, she called the shop instead of his cell.

"Vintage British, how can I help you?"

"Hi, Thean."

"Hey, Cassie, how are you?"

"I'm good. Is Eli there?"

"Not right now. Want me to have him call you?"

"Yes, please. Thanks, Thean."

"No problem. Talk to you later."

Sitting at her desk, she tried to calm her nerves. It seemed as if Eli was avoiding her, but she couldn't imagine why. Cassie wanted to be there for him and Addison. But she was being shut out.

The rest of the day flew by in a blur of meetings and emails, with no word from Eli before she left the office. Even the success of the presentation did little to boost her mood.

On the way home, he called.

"Eli!" Cassie's voice rose. "I've been trying to reach you."

"I know. I needed some space." His voice was stiff.

"From Me? Really?" She took a deep breath. The phone trembled in her hand. "Please don't shut me out."

"It's complicated." There was tension in his voice.

"Why? Is it because Tandy doesn't want me involved?" The confusion whirling around her head came tumbling out.

He emitted a sound that could only be described as someone being strangled over the phone. Before she could ask if he was okay, he said, "You're already involved." His words were so low Cassie almost didn't catch them.

"I don't understand. I haven't talked to you in two days."

"I know. I don't know how to handle this."

"*What's this?* Is Addison okay?"

"Tandy won't let me talk to her."

"When are you coming home?"

"About that..."

"What about it? Eli, talk to me."

The silence hung between them like an invisible

wall. The tension was palpable. And Cassie's anxiety was ratcheting up to a level that had her eyelid twitching.

"Tandy claims you abused Addison."

"Whoa. What?" Cassie yanked the car into the nearest parking lot and slammed on the brakes. "Where the hell did that come from?"

"She claims it happened the day we went to the Raptor Center."

"How? That was a public park." Her head throbbed as she scrambled to run the events of the day through her mind. The migraine hadn't released its grip.

"Wish I understood more. I'm just going with what Tandy said, and what the social worker told me."

"Eli, we need to talk. When are you coming home?"

"That's just it. According to the social worker, I can't."

"Can't? What the hell does that mean? Please explain. I deserve that much!"

"She told me if I didn't move out, I would lose all visitation privileges with Addison."

"How can they tell you where to live?"

"That's just what she said. It's for Addison's safety."

"This is bull—shit." She snapped, her composure slipping.

"I know."

"Pl—Please come home. We need to talk." She closed her eyes as fresh tears built.

"I don't know. I don't want to risk it." His voice held no emotion.

"Fine, I'll meet you somewhere. Please." Cassie sobbed.

"Please don't cry, Cassie. I'm so sorry."

"You—You—don't beli—eve her? Do you?" she asked in between sobs.

"I don't believe her," he said in a soft voice.

"Please come home. If you don't, the investigators will think you believe this, and you're not standing by me. If you don't—" She hiccupped, "I could go to jail! Don't you understand?" She sobbed harder, unable to stop. "I did nothing wrong."

"Please calm down."

"How can I be calm?" Her voice rose. "I'm being accused of—" She couldn't even say the words. "—of hurting Addison and you tell me to be calm." Hysteria was only inches away, smothering the last thread of her composure.

"Cassie. Please don't fall apart on me."

"Too late," she whispered.

She hung up the phone and sat in her car, her head resting against the steering wheel, sobbing until there was nothing left.

CHAPTER 11

A Formal Investigation

Cassie

C assie cried herself to sleep. It took two more days before Eli agreed to come home, but she was grateful. Things remained stiff between them, but at least he was standing by her.

A week after she'd found Eli's note, she came home to a blinking light on the answering machine. She pressed play, kicking off her shoes from another long day.

"Hello, this message is for Cassandra Flynn. This is Detective Erin Groves of the Durham Police

Department. I'm investigating an allegation of abuse, and would like to interview you. Please call me at—" Cassie paused the message to scribble down the details.

Calling back, she spoke with an assistant and scheduled an appointment for the next day after work.

Eli drove her to the police station. On the way, they talked about her fears.

"I'm terrified," she said. "A sexual abuse accusation could destroy my life, even without proof." Just the hint of it tainted a person. It had the power to change lives forever. Cassie trembled as these thoughts tumbled through her head.

"I'm still shocked at the accusation," Eli admitted.

After they arrived and checked in, they sat holding hands.

The detective came out to receive them and led them down a long hallway and into her office, a small, white room with a desk and a narrow couch against the opposite wall.

They sat with their hands entwined. Eli gave a gentle squeeze, offering his silent support.

"We received a report that a three-and-a-half-year-old child was sexually molested by you, Ms.

Flynn. It's my responsibility to look into these allegations."

"I understand." Cassie's voice cracked.

"Tandy—my ex—informed me last week that she took my daughter to the doctor, and he found evidence of abuse," Eli said. "And some social worker called right after telling me to end my relationship with Cassie and move out. Otherwise, I would be prevented from seeing Addison."

"Interesting. Can you give me the name of the person you talked to?" Detective Groves asked.

"I have it at home. Can I call you with it?"

"That will be fine. Now, Cassie, tell me about the event in question."

Cassie nodded. "We were at the Raptor Center. I offered to take Addison to the women's bathroom. That way Eli wouldn't have to take her into the men's. We were inside for less than ten minutes. The line was long." Her voice was clipped.

"Tell me about that."

"The bathroom was busy. I took her into one of the largest stalls. I helped her slip off her shoes, and then she pulled off her leggings and pull-up. Then I held her up under the arms, so she could slip on a new pull-up, then her pants and shoes. We washed our hands and went to join Eli outside."

"Did you wipe her or touch her in any way?"

"No! She had only peed. It was a simple exchange of the wet pull-up for a dry one." She took a shaky breath, not meaning to raise her voice.

"Okay," Detective Groves said, scribbling furiously in the notebook on her lap. "Do you have any idea how this allegation came about?"

"Tandy found out about us—that we live together," Cassie said. The tension in her shoulders was painfully tight.

"What do you mean, she found out?"

"We started dating earlier this year, and Eli moved in a few months ago," Cassie said.

"Tandy and I went to court recently, and the judge ordered an increased visitation schedule for me. Something she tried to sideline many times, dragging it on for months," Eli added.

"I figured it was something along those lines," Detective Groves said. Her voice was gentle. "I should start by letting you know that I've already spoken to the doctor and had an interesting conversation with Tandy Heaver."

Cassie sucked in her breath. Her shoulders tightened even further. Terrible anxiety flowed through her all over again. "Okay, and?"

"You should know the doctor found no physical

evidence, and he informed Tandy of that while she was in his office—"

"That's not what they said," Eli interrupted.

"All I can say is the social worker was misinformed. The doctor performed a complete physical exam and looked for any sign of physical and sexual abuse. The two forms of abuse most times exist together."

Cassie flinched and blinked back tears. A ringing in her ears began.

Eli stiffened next to her as the blood drained from his face.

"There is nothing wrong with her physically and she exhibits none of the typical signs associated with any abuse."

"That exam sounds awful for Addison," Cassie said, her voice filled with horror. A shiver ran down her back.

"Yes, the doctor was extra careful under the circumstances. He explained that, in his opinion, the situation had a forced feel to it, or an agenda behind the visit. He also conveyed the mother did the talking, and the child said little."

"Well, why did he call social services then, if he thought there was something off with the situation?" Eli asked. His tone was haughty as he sat up straighter in the seat.

"The doctor didn't. Tandy asked for an investigation, telling them the doctor told her to make the call."

Cassie's breath came out in a whoosh.

"Tandy is obviously not well versed in how the process works. With any evidence of physical or sexual abuse, a doctor is required by law to make a report. The doctor told her he found nothing wrong with Addison. He informed her there was nothing further to be done, and he did not tell her to call CPS herself."

"I don't understand," Eli said. "Why would the social worker tell me there was, and that I needed to end my relationship with Cassie if I wanted to see my daughter again?"

"I don't know, Mr. Tetrick," the detective said, as confusion crossed her face. "I wasn't aware anyone had contacted you. There are two counties involved. Information must have crossed."

"Where does that leave us?" Eli asked.

"Well," the detective said, "after a long talk with Mrs. Heaver, I have to admit I didn't find her account credible. Her story was inconsistent and differed from what the doctor told me."

Cassie clenched Eli's hand. Her stomach did a somersault.

"Now, I believe I have a better understanding about what prompted this allegation. I also have a clear picture about the events that transpired with your daughter. The stage of potty training where she wears pull-ups and not diapers changes the situation."

"How?" Cassie exhaled a breath she hadn't realized she'd been holding. The tension in her shoulders made it painful.

"I want to understand, because frankly, after the way this whole situation has played out, I have little faith in the system."

Detective Groves turned to Cassie and said, "I do not believe you caused any harm to Mr. Tetrick's daughter."

The dam burst. Deep and powerful sobs racked her body while Eli held her. The relief was overwhelming. She couldn't contain it.

Eli stroked her arm as she asked, "Where do we go from here?"

Hiccups had begun, and her body convulsed involuntarily.

"I will send a report stating there was no abuse,

and the investigation is complete, and I'll also make sure Unity County gets a copy."

"I don't need to move out?" Eli asked. His shoulders hadn't relaxed.

Cassie interrupted. "I won't go to jail?"

"No, of course not. Once the investigation is closed, that should be the end of it."

"What about us? What can we do to prevent this in the future?"

"That I'm afraid I don't have an answer for," Detective Groves' voice was solemn and full of sympathy.

"Thank you." More tears welled in her eyes.

"For everything," Eli added. Relief flooded his face. For the first time, genuine emotion escaped his unshakable demeanor.

"Just doing my job. I'm happy everything will work out for you."

Detective Groves walked them out of the police department. They were in better spirits than they had been in almost two weeks.

"Good luck, you two," Groves said. "Take care."

THE FOLLOWING WEEK, CASSIE JOINED ELI IN court. They hoped to prevent his visitation rights from being rescinded due to the accusations. She had been to court before, even testified, but never because of some crazed, half-baked accusation. The butterflies in her stomach seemed determined to escape if their fluttering was any sign. Detective Groves had believed in her innocence. Now she needed to have faith the judge would as well.

The small courtroom was packed, every seat in the gallery occupied. It was almost stifling. The air hummed with the sounds of multiple hushed conversations. For a town with a population of less than five thousand people, it was surprising how much family drama existed within its boundaries. The room went quiet when a tall, dark-haired sheriff's deputy stood to face them. The silence was almost deafening when the animated conversations ceased at once.

"All Rise, the Family Court of Unity County is in session, Honorable Judge Westerhouse presiding," the bailiff called, as the judge entered from a door to the side of the room. "You may be seated." The judge arranged himself behind the bench and the proceedings began.

At their turn, Eli moved to the other side of the

divider to sit at the worn wooden table on the right, as Tandy sat to the left of the room.

Cassie remained in the first row, directly behind Eli.

The judge read Tandy's declaration and pursed his lips. "These are serious allegations. I see there is a request to put a hold on visitations." The judge paused and peered over his glasses in Eli's direction. His glare reached Cassie in the front row. It made her squirm in her seat.

"The investigation is complete, Your Honor. The allegations were unfounded," Eli said.

Sitting in the front row, Cassie had a clear view as the representative from CPS turned to Tandy. Both women wore shocked expressions and appeared surprised at this turn of events.

"Your Honor, may I have a quick recess to step out and confirm this?" the social worker requested.

"Yes, you may."

The social worker and Tandy walked out of the courtroom, and an oppressive silence filled the room. Eli sat down in an empty seat next to Cassie. She reached over and put her hand in his and squeezed without saying a word. Fifteen minutes passed before Tandy returned with the social worker. Her head was down, and she met no one's gaze.

"Your Honor, we would like to withdraw our request considering the findings."

"Granted. Case dismissed." The judge banged his gavel. And that was the end. The air escaped Cassie's lungs with an audible whoosh.

Tandy and the social worker walked out as soon as the judge lifted his gavel. Tandy was speaking at rapid-fire speed. Her hands flew around almost as fast. She was clearly unhappy it had not gone in her favor. The social worker seemed unable to tamper Tandy's non-stop rant, and it persisted until they made it to the lobby. Walking out a short distance behind them, they watched the exchange continue.

"I can only hope we can put it behind us now," Cassie said.

"I think she's got her talons drawn now that things didn't go her way, both with us and the case," Eli replied, "and that makes me nervous. I may need to hire the lawyer I talked to last year."

"I hope you're wrong, Eli," Cassie said, as they watched Tandy storm off.

CHAPTER 12

Another Baby Girl

Eli

Eli was in the shop checking on the shipment he'd just received. The parts he needed for his current restoration project were all there. He hummed along with the radio as he inspected them.

He was about to head out to check in at the front desk when Thean caught up to him.

"Tandy just called."

"Ugh. What now?"

"She just said to have you call her."

"Yeah, I'll get right on that." Eli didn't bother to reign in the sarcasm.

Thean chuckled and shook his head. "At least she didn't sound pissy for a change."

"That, my friend, is not always a good omen." Eli sighed. Still furious about her accusations against Cassie, he figured the less he dealt with her, the less chance he had of exploding on her.

"True. Anyway, I'm heading out for lunch. Can you cover the front?" Thean said, pointing a thumb over his shoulder. "Want anything?"

"No problem. Can you bring me back a sandwich?"

"Of course." Thean sauntered out. The phone rang as the door closed behind Thean.

"Vintage British."

"Eli, it's me."

He groaned. He should have expected Tandy would keep calling until she found him.

"What can I do for you?" He snapped a pencil in half between his fingers. Just hearing her voice grated on his last nerve.

"I wanted to call you with the good news."

"Okay, what's up?"

"Savannah and Addison will have another sister."

He rolled his eyes. This was the first time he'd talked to Tandy in months. The exchanges with Addison were now taking place with Tandy's mother, leaving no interaction between them.

"Eli, did you hear me? I'm having a girl."

"Good for you. Luke's?"

"Don't be a jerk, Eli."

"I'm sorry, but you have to admit, it's an honest question."

"Yes, she is Luke's," Tandy replied in a huff.

"Why are you calling *me*?" Scratching his head, he couldn't fathom his need to know.

"I wanted to be the one to tell you."

Why would I give a rat's ass?

"I've got to go. Give my love to the girls." He disconnected the call before she could say anything else.

With a heavy thump, he dropped into the chair behind the counter. The call took the wind out of his sails. Talking to her always did. He didn't understand her need to tell him about the baby. It wasn't like he cared. Why was she obsessed with trying to draw him back in? He was still staring at the ceiling when Thean returned with the sandwiches.

"What did Tandy want?" Thean asked, dropping the sandwiches on the counter. He dug through the bag and handed one over to Eli.

"How did you know I'd talked to her?"

"Seriously? It's written all over your face. You look like you just ate a rotten pickle." He tore open the sandwich wrapper.

"That bad, huh? Yeah, I talked to her. She's an odd one."

"What's new?"

"She wanted to tell me she was having a girl."

"Oh, boy. Not yours, I hope." Thean smirked, devouring his lunch.

"Funny." He glared at his friend. "No, Luke's. I wouldn't be surprised if that's the reason for their quick marriage." He trailed off, picking up his sandwich.

"And she wanted you to know? Why?"

"My thoughts exactly."

"Hope for your sake it won't give Cassie any ideas about babies."

"Oh, that's the last thing I need." Eli rolled his eyes.

Thean chuckled, wadded up his lunch remains, and stood. "I don't know. Not everything has an ulterior motive."

Eli scoffed. "You don't know Tandy. She's brewing something. She always is."

He unwrapped his sandwich and took a huge bite, hoping to remove Tandy from his mind.

CHAPTER 13

Engagement

Cassie

O nce again, Cassie and Eli found themselves back in court. One would have thought with Tandy's marriage to Luke, celebrating Addison's fourth birthday, and the birth of her third child, she would be too busy to cause drama. But, without warning, she'd called Eli, pissed off about the visitation schedule.

The morning was overcast, with a sharp chill in the air. Cassie dreaded appearing in court again so soon. Things with Eli's ex had not improved as much as she hoped.

"...Court of Unity County is in session... presiding," the bailiff said. Cassie studied the floor as he brought the court to session. She'd missed most of the bailiff's speech, distracted by her pulse raging in her eardrums. She looked up as the judge entered, his black robe billowing around him as he climbed the steps to his seat.

"You may be seated." The sounds of creaking wood filled the room as everyone sat at once.

She wiped her clammy hands on her slacks as she slid into the wooden chair. Her purse almost slid out of her grasp as she tried to set it on her legs without spilling its contents. The edge of the chair bit into her legs. She sat stiffly, watching the proceedings with a growing sense of doom.

Eli sat at the table in front of her with his new lawyer.

"I'm sorry, Mr. Chaiken, but your client should have noticed this before now." The judge reviewed the papers in his hand and then looked at the lawyer. "I won't order Ms. Heaver to change her plans the day before the holiday."

"But, Your Honor, according to the papers and my client, the mother had the holiday last year."

"I understand, but you waited too long to bring it before the court. I sympathize with your client that Thanksgiving was omitted from the final document."

Chaiken set the file on the table and took his seat.

"Motion denied." The judge banged his gavel.

Cassie hated that sound.

Eli glanced at his lawyer as the judge took his leave. Tandy hadn't bothered to make an appearance.

"Of course, what the hell did I expect?" Eli lamented as he marched out the heavy wooden double doors at the back of the court. They swooshed closed with a bang behind him. Chaiken didn't respond. He just patted Eli on the shoulder.

They left the lawyer on the chipped stone steps at the front of the courthouse, and Eli drove home fuming.

The more Cassie thought about Eli's ex-wife, the more agitated she became. By the time they made it home, they were both in a foul mood. He tossed his court file on the counter in the kitchen. The file slid halfway across the surface before it skidded to a stop.

Walking to the refrigerator, she pulled out the leftover marinara sauce and poured it into a pan on the stove. She stirred the sauce while he poured wine.

She had warned him the judge might refuse his eleventh-hour request. But she said nothing now.

"Today was a complete waste of time." Eli hefted his clearly exhausted body onto one of the bar stools at the counter. He sipped his drink.

"I'm surprised the judge didn't at least change the visitation order to address the mistake."

"Yeah. The judge was a jerk."

Furious tension built up in her shoulders as she thought about how the latest crap had transpired. Tandy got angry they would get three weekends in a row because of Thanksgiving. She had apparently pulled out her copy of the visitation schedule and left a message telling Eli he wasn't getting the holiday, and there was nothing he could do about it, since it wasn't even in the visitation order.

While they both were angry, given that it was last minute, it wasn't much of a surprise the judge refused to make changes. Still, Cassie's blood boiled thinking about Tandy's games.

"Tandy's message said they went to Luke's family for the holiday. As usual, everything goes her way," Eli ranted.

"I'm sorry, sweetheart. This sucks." She

splashed more wine into his glass and handed it back to him with a kiss. They had an early and quiet dinner, their moods bleak.

Afterward, Eli headed for the couch to watch a movie while she changed.

The disappointment was palpable, neither able to shake it. Cassie decided she needed to do something drastic to change it. She had expected the possibility of the judge not granting Eli's request, but she hadn't been prepared for it to crush him like this.

In their bedroom, she exchanged her slacks for something silky and sexy, hoping it would distract Eli from his black mood. Opening the top drawer of her lingerie chest, she reached in and grabbed a square box. The rings they had picked out together, custom designed, had arrived the day before. There was no plan yet to exchange them. They'd discussed getting married and had ordered the rings, but that was as far as they had gotten.

Opening the box, she gazed at his ring. Closing it, she kissed the top and whispered, "Wish me luck." She took the box and slid it into the middle of her sexy lingerie for him to find.

"What on earth?" He chuckled as she came into

the room. He had lit the fireplace and the candles on the mantle. It bathed the room in a soft, flickering glow.

Cassie blushed and shrugged. Facing him, in a little black lacy thing with the square box's sharp angles bulging from it, she spun a clumsy pirouette. He laughed again and pulled them down onto the floor, kissing her with renewed passion.

Her only purpose at that point was to lift his spirits. She succeeded, considering it was the first time he'd laughed in days. After she had slipped the ring on his finger, he kissed her with such hunger that her vision blurred. Her mind whirled with desire as her body ached for his touch.

"Wait here," he said as he pulled away from her. "I have a surprise for you as well." He kissed the top of her nose and left her lying on a blanket, hastily snagged from the couch in the candlelit room. She stared at the flickering orange and blue flames of the gas fireplace.

He returned with a ceramic bowl of strawberries and a can of whipped cream.

"Ooh, whipped cream." She giggled and smiled up at him as he knelt beside her. Her attention was on him as he untied his shoes, pulling them off.

Grabbing the can of whipped cream, she wrapped her lips around the nozzle. Tilting it back, something hard fell in her mouth, sliding across her tongue, surrounded by the gooey cream confection.

She choked, stunned by the realization Eli had slipped her ring around the nozzle. He grabbed her, turned her on her side, and pounded on her back. Each thump was like he was breaking her spine before she coughed it out. She almost choked again when she saw the ring on the floor, and him grinning at her like an idiot.

"I'm thinking a trip to the emergency room wouldn't be an ideal end to the evening."

Her skin was hot and slick. In a single moment, his attempt at romance had come close to becoming a disaster. *Christ. I almost swallowed my engagement ring!* She could hardly believe it.

"So, is that a yes?" he asked.

"Yes!"

She was laughing as he reached over and took her face in his hands and kissed her again with such a force it made her dizzy. He kissed each shoulder as he slid off the delicate straps. As the soft satin skimmed down her breasts to her belly, he covered the exposed skin with more soft kisses. They made slow, consuming love, the kisses and motions taking their mind off everything except each passionate touch. They lay on the floor, wrapped in each other's arms, their hunger sated as they fell asleep.

THE NEXT MORNING, CASSIE CALLED HER PARENTS in Florida to give them the news. Her mother was ecstatic, and her father congratulated them both. Afterward, they drove over to Eli's parents' house. They would spend the holiday with them and tell them of the engagement in person.

As they walked into the kitchen, Eli put his arm around his mother. "I asked Cassie to marry me last night."

"It's about time," Linnane said.

"Mom," Eli glared at her.

"I'm sorry, but you know how I feel about the two of you not being married. Think of the example you're setting for Addison, and now you can start a family. I'd like more grandchildren."

Eli shook his head and glanced over at his father, who shrugged out of his wife's line of view.

"We are happy for you," Linnane said.

Eli reached for Cassie's hand and gave it a small

squeeze. This wasn't the first time his mother had made comments about their living arrangements. The men watched the game while Linnane and Cassie sat at the breakfast table, drinking tea, and chatting about dinner preparations, when the neighbors, Dave, and Isobel, stopped by for an impromptu visit. Cassie had never met them. After the introductions, Eli's father, Bryan, turned to him, said, "Eli, let's show Dave the new project you're working on. It's a sixty-three Jag XKE." The three men walked out to the garage to look at the latest car project Eli and Cassie had driven.

"Isobel, the kids *finally* got engaged," Linnane turned to her friend and poured her a cup of tea.

Isobel looked over at Cassie and then down at the ring, and scrunched up her nose. "I can't fathom the desire for such an ostentatious ring."

"It's not as expensive as you might think," Cassie said. Her face flushed with embarrassment as she slid her hand underneath the table.

"I suppose you intend a lavish, showy wedding as well?" Isobel asked, ignoring Cassie's response.

"I'm hoping for the church," Linnane hinted.

Cassie remained mute. Unwilling to give more fuel, for fear of what other nastiness would spew forth from this stranger.

"In retrospect," Isobel continued, "if I'd known then what I know now, I wouldn't have spent money on a fancy ring and a big wedding production. It's such an expensive thing and a waste of money you could put towards something more important. I would have bought a bigger house, giving my boys each their own bedroom."

After her little tirade wound down, their conversation shifted to plans for dinner. It remained between Isobel and Linnane while Cassie sipped her tea in silence.

A few minutes later, Isobel excused herself and went to find her husband. Eli and his father came in and saw the hurt looks exchanged between Cassie and Linnane.

"What's wrong?" Bryan asked. He looked at his wife.

"Isobel had an opinion about Cassie's ring."

"And the wedding," Cassie added, her head down.

"She was a tad harsh and I'm afraid Cassie's feelings are hurt."

"I guess she based it on their new circumstances," Bryan groaned.

"Isobel's ill and can't work anymore. Now

they're struggling financially." Linnane poured more tea as she spoke.

"I understand she has different priorities now. But she also has a family. She probably shouldn't have had four children if she couldn't provide for them," Eli muttered as he sat beside Cassie.

She was grateful he came to her defense instead of agreeing with the others that her engagement ring and wedding plans were squandering their money.

"It's not that simple, Eli. A mother never regrets having children, no matter what happens. Instead, we focus on what more we might have sacrificed."

"I understand, but it's hypocritical to tell Cassie her dreams are wrong. She should have kept her misery to herself. There was no reason to inflict her personal beliefs on us."

"Eli, the two of you haven't made it easy on yourselves. Living together out of wedlock…"

Eli held his hand up, stopping his mother short. "Mom, don't start on that again. I tried to do the 'proper' thing with Tandy and look where it got me."

"I get all that, Linnane. I really do. Who knows, in twenty years I may see things her way. Maybe it says more about my priorities than hers, but it seems petty to begrudge someone else's happiness," Cassie said, trying to head off another argument about them living in sin.

"Time will tell," Linnane replied.

Cassie let out a sigh. She was done trying to find a silver lining from this evening.

CHAPTER 14

First Christmas

Cassie

Cassie and Eli got caught up in the whirlwind of holiday celebrations. It was the first week of December before they told their friends and the rest of their family their good news.

It was Christmas day when Tandy learned of it. She dropped Addison off at the apartment. Eli hadn't had the chance to tell Addison yet. They agreed not to tell her on the phone. When Tandy walked in the front door, the tension in Cassie's shoulders tripled.

"Hi Daddy and Cassie," Addison said.

"Merry Christmas honey, go put your stuff away," Eli said before kissing the top of her head. Cassie smiled at her.

Addison ran down the hall to her room to drop off her overnight bag. Tandy stood stiffly by the front door, waiting for Addison to return. Tandy's husband, Luke, remained down in the car with Savannah and the new baby, Quinby.

"I'm glad we were in town and able to drop her off to make it easier for you. You do that for me so often," Tandy gushed at Eli.

Cassie turned her attention to the room, to the brightly colored decorations that adorned the small Douglas fir in the corner. Underneath lay a massive pile of wrapped gifts. A small leather couch and love seat faced a large off-brand television on a small stand. She tried to picture how the room looked through Tandy's eyes. When she looked back, Tandy was studying her hands.

"You're engaged." Surprise and anger laced her words.

Before Cassie could say anything, Eli responded. "Yes, last month."

"Hmm." Tandy continued to stare daggers at Cassie's hand.

"Mama. Mama. Come see my room." Addison called from the hallway.

Tandy stalked past Cassie. As Tandy walked out of the room, Cassie met Eli's gaze in silent communication. A few moments later, Addison and Tandy came back together.

"You decorated a room for her." Tandy again spoke only to Eli.

"Yes, we wanted her to be comfortable here," he said.

Tandy kneeled in front of Addison and reached for her. "Give me a hug," Tandy said, squeezing her tight. "Have a good Christmas."

"You too, mommy."

"I'll see you in a week, okay? I love you."

"Okay mommy, I love you too."

Tandy looked up at Eli, gave a slight nod, then walked out.

As Eli closed the door behind Tandy, Cassie said, "Well, that was tense."

"Yeah, a bit uncomfortable. Let's get out of here." He turned to Addison. "Grab your jacket. We're going to Nona's house."

"Okay, Daddy," Addison said, sprinting to her bedroom.

Eli knelt to gather the gifts underneath the tree.

Cassie switched off the coffeepot and returned with the two bottles of wine sitting on the counter at the same time as Addison, holding her coat in her hands.

Addison was quiet in the backseat, engrossed with a new toy the entire drive to Eli's parents' house.

"I have to admit, I'm excited today. It's my first Christmas with her since the divorce!" Eli said as he turned down the radio. "Last year, I dropped off gifts but couldn't stay because Tandy was still furious." He checked the rearview mirror, glancing at Addison in the back seat.

"Is she asleep?"

"Yes, she's zonked out."

"I'm glad we have today, and it's great we'll have her next week as well." She reached for his hand.

"Yes, what should we do for fun? I haven't wrapped my head around the idea of an entire week with her."

"Well, I thought we'd take her to the Museum of Art over in Charlotte to see the Egyptian artifacts exhibit, and maybe a show. Addison might like the Fox and the Hound movie."

"That works," Eli smiled. "I know my mom

wants to spend at least a day with her while she's here."

When they arrived at Eli's family's home, there was a full house. He kissed his mother on the cheek before visiting with the brood. Bryant's extended family came for the holiday. With her purse placed on a chair and the wine on the kitchen table, Cassie rolled up her sleeves to help her soon to be mother-in-law.

"Linnane, what can I do?"

"Nothing. I have it all under control."

"How about making the appetizers or snacks?" Cassie asked.

"I've got those covered. If you could make the mimosas, we'll go sit and open gifts."

"Perfect."

"The glasses are in the curio; the champagne is in the refrigerator next to the juices."

Cassie mixed up a batch of mimosas, set the glass pitcher on the tray, and walked into the other room to get the glasses out of the cabinet.

Addison zoomed past her, causing the tray to jangle as she carried the mimosas into the parlor.

"Addison, no running inside," Cassie called out. Addison stopped in her tracks and walked the rest of the way.

Eli's mother was right behind her. "Oh, she's okay."

Cassie cringed but bit her tongue to keep the peace, though she didn't like the idea of Addison dashing around the house. Once everyone was in the room, Bryant handed out the gifts. Cassie relaxed cross-legged on the floor as Eli sat on the edge of a sofa. Within moments, Addison had an overflowing pile of gifts at her feet. She tore into each paper with an excited flourish.

Eli handed Cassie a large, flat gift. The wrapping was professionally done, beautiful and precise. Cassie set it on her lap and unwrapped it, gasping at a framed lithograph of a fair-haired angel child with soft white outstretched wings encased in a dark cherry wood picture frame.

Addison scooted closer and looked up as Cassie turned the picture outward. "That looks like me!" Addison squealed, clasping her hands. She bounced on her folded legs.

"Yes, it does. A little Addy angel," Cassie said, as she wrapped her arm around Addison and gave her a hug.

"I like it," Addison said as she hugged Cassie back.

"It's beautiful, Cassie," Linnane said.

Tears welled up in her eyes. It was a thoughtful gift. The picture was lovely, and knowing that Addison liked it made it even more special.

"The first time we laid eyes on it, I mentioned it reminded me of Addison. I didn't think he was paying any attention," she said.

"I was," Eli said.

"Thank you. I know the perfect place for this." She leaned up and kissed him. Somehow, the watch she had given him paled compared to this thoughtful and generous gift.

The holiday sped by. As the sun set, everyone packed their things into their cars and said their goodbyes.

CHAPTER 15

Another Day, Another Allegation

Eli

The Christmas break had been a whirlwind. Dinner with Eli's family, two Disney movies, and, for the last day of Addison's visit, they checked out the Egyptian collection at the North Carolina Museum of Art. While most of the artifacts would not interest Addison, she had wanted to see more pictures of royal cats, like Seshat. She was enamored with Cassie's cat.

Hand in hand, Cassie and Addison walked over to the pottery section of the exhibit behind Eli.

"That's pretty." Addison pointed to a large earthenware jar that stood on a base in the center of the room.

"Yes, it is, and it's really old," Eli said.

As Addison led Cassie around the small, enclosed room that housed the museum's permanent collection of the Egyptian artifacts, she pointed to the items she liked.

"Can I take this one home?" Addison asked. She stood in front of a collection of Canopic jars. The head of Hapi had caught her attention. Her eyes were bright, and her voice full of innocence. She had the enthusiasm only a young child is blessed with.

"Honey, this belongs to the museum. We can't take this home with us," Eli said.

"But I like the monkey." Addison bit her lip.

"How about if we visit the gift shop? They might have one you like more?" Cassie suggested.

Addison's face brightened and distracted. She enjoyed the rest of the exhibit.

In the gift shop, they didn't find a Canopic jar she liked, but settled on having her name printed in Egyptian hieroglyphs instead. They had it framed to hang on her bedroom wall.

As Eli held a giggling Addison up to place the

new picture on her wall, he laughed. "Your bedroom is certainly a hodgepodge of things now."

"I think it suits her. What do you think, Addy? Do you like your room?" Cassie asked.

"I like it." Addison squirmed and giggled as Eli tickled her.

Cassie laughed and kissed her cheek, turning them toward the east wall. "Which wall do you like best? Disney princesses and their princes, or the angel wall?" Using the child's hand, she pointed to the third wall, the one where they had just hung the Egyptian picture. "Or the Egyptian wall?"

"All of them!" Addison squealed. Eli had her flying through the air like an airplane before sliding her onto her bed. Cassie chuckles as she watches from the doorway.

"Night, Daddy. Love you."

"Love you too, baby." Eli tucked her in and kissed her goodnight.

"Night little one. We'll see you in the morning," Cassie said.

"Night, Cassie."

Two weeks had passed since the holiday, when the shrill of the phone filled the air. Eli had just walked into the kitchen as Cassie pulled the chicken from the oven. He kissed her cheek before he answered it.

"Hello." Eli said in a chipper mood.

"Who is it?" Cassie mouthed.

"Yes, Tandy," he said. He looked up and rolled his eyes as Cassie grinned. He pressed the volume button up as he rested against the counter. She walked over and leaned next to him so she could listen to the call. He put his fingers to his lips, and she nodded. They are used to this method of communication.

"Are you sure it's a good idea to marry Cassie, all things considered?"

Eli let out a heavy sigh. "Yes, as a matter of fact, I do."

"Fine."

"Was there anything else?" Eli asked.

"I just wanted you to know I talked to DSS yesterday."

"For what now?"

Cassie put her hand on his arm as his shoulders tensed.

"For kicking Addison's bedroom door and

hitting her."

"Where the hell did that come from?" His voice raised an octave and his whole body stiffened. He was fed up with her half-baked accusations.

Cassie stared at Eli's horror-struck face. It was surreal.

"Addy said you dragged her down the hall by her hair."

"I would never!" The agitation in his voice made it sharper than usual.

"That's not what she told me," Tandy responded in a haughty tone.

"When did this *alleged* abuse happen?"

"While she was with you for Christmas."

"This is complete bullshit, and you know it," Eli growled.

Cassie reached for him, wrapped an arm around him, and pressed into him. They stood together in silence and listened.

"I saw the bedroom door, Eli," came the cold, matter-of-fact reply.

Eli looked at Cassie. She shrugged.

"What do you mean?" Eli asked.

"When I came in and saw her room. There was a hole in the door."

Eli raised his brow. "If you noticed the door, it

couldn't have happened after you dropped her off. This is just more of your crap because I'm engaged to Cassie."

"It has nothing to do with that!" Tandy's snarl was fierce.

Tears pooled in Cassie's eyes. Once again, Tandy had created drama to fit her agenda.

"This was my first year to have Addison for the holidays since the divorce. You just had to screw it up, didn't you?" he said, anger overwhelming his voice.

"Of course not." Tandy's voice was defiant.

"This is just another round of your stupid pissing matches." He hung up the phone.

Cassie stood there, her hand in his. He looked like a kettle ready to blow.

"That god damned, insufferable, psychotic, bitch!"

Flinching, she took a step back. "Take a deep breath."

"She's concocted another crazy-assed story to punish us."

"We'll talk to Chaiken and see what he can do."

"God damn this shit. I'm sick of fighting with her over everything."

"I'm sorry, babe."

He stalked out of the kitchen.

TWO DAYS AFTER THE CALL FROM TANDY, ELI strode into the apartment and tossed the mail on the counter as he kissed her cheek. He had a letter open in his hand.

"Well, here we go again," he said in a sing-song voice. Cassie stood behind him and looked over his shoulder as they read the letter together in silence.

DEAR MR. TETRICK,

The Department of Social Services has completed its physical abuse investigation and has found the allegations of abuse on Addison Tetrick inconclusive. We could not prove the allegations to be neither true nor false.

The Child Abuse Central Index at the Department of Justice has received a copy of this incident. The Law requires this when the allegations are either found to be true or inconclusive.

Sincerely,
Lisa Strapp
CPS Social Worker

. . .

"What will you do?" Cassie said.

"I don't know. There is nothing here about a rebuttal or an appeal. Just the obvious fact this social worker did a half-assed, incomplete job, not bothering to talk to any witnesses other than Tandy," Eli snapped.

"We need to fax this to the lawyer."

"I can't believe this damn social worker didn't bother to look into it. She decided the investigation was complete and determined it 'inconclusive' based on a single interview with Tandy."

The top of the second page listed a report number, saying the investigation of suspected child abuse was completed pursuant to General Statutes §7B-101 and §7B-301.

Eli read the first paragraph aloud, "law enforcement agencies, probation departments, county welfare agencies, and district attorneys access this index when conducting investigations of child abuse. Court investigators and licensing agencies also access it to screen individuals for child placements." He looked at Cassie. "What does that even mean?"

"I'm not sure it would affect you from a professional standpoint. It's not like you are a teacher or work with children. But it means we're screwed from becoming foster parents."

"This isn't about that. Tandy doesn't want to hurt me professionally or she wouldn't get any more money out of me. It's about stopping me from seeing Addison. You know it is."

Looking at his oil-stained hands, he tossed the letter on the counter. "I need a shower," he said, and stalked out of the room.

The following afternoon, there was a knock on the front door. Cassie opened it to find a short Asian man on the porch, wearing a pair of black slacks and a button up white shirt. He was in his mid-forties with shiny black hair, a few strands of silver at his temples.

"Hello, Mr. Tetrick?" he asked as Eli walked up behind Cassie.

"Yes."

The man showed a badge identifying him as Alan Lee, a DSS social worker for Durham County.

"Hello, Mr. Lee. I'm a little confused," Eli said.

"I'm here to investigate an allegation of child abuse."

"I assumed that. My ex-wife called, and a letter came from a social worker in Unity County. The letter informed me the investigation was complete and results submitted to a national database."

"I don't understand why they would do that. It's only been about a week since the complaint was filed."

"Come in, please." Cassie stepped away from the door.

"Thank you," he said as he came in and sat on the love seat. Mr. Lee explained the National Index. "The database is statewide and is used mainly for reference."

"Is there a way to get my name removed?" Eli asked.

"The only way I know is to have the social worker who entered it remove it."

"How can she close a case and submit my name without a conversation with me, much less a thorough investigation?"

"I don't know. I'm just here to make a report based on my findings."

Cassie sat quietly, fuming at this intrusion into their lives again. The social worker had sidestepped the question, the same thing the social worker from the other county had done.

"How can we refute the first report?" Eli asked.

Again, the social worker avoided responding.

Cassie sat quietly while her insides coiled into a knot. This nightmare was happening because of a jealous, unstable woman. But unlike before where Detective Groves took the time to talk to both sides and do an actual investigation, this time, the decision was final, without any effort. "Mr. Lee, here is a copy of a letter from the landlord explaining the damaged door." She handed over the document. "He offered to fix the damage when I moved in, but he just hasn't had time to fix it."

"I see. I understand the allegations said you caused it."

Eli nodded. "That's what my ex would like you to believe."

"These are not the first accusations made by Tandy. After you see the door for yourself, maybe you would like to go to Eli's parents' home and meet with them, and with Addison. You will have a better opportunity to get the full story, not just our side of it," Cassie said.

"I appreciate that," Mr. Lee said.

"We have nothing to hide. This is exactly like her last accusation. The last time was also right after court, and the judge granted my motions, not hers." Eli ran his hand through his hair.

Cassie shifted in her seat to face the social

worker as she spoke. "The calls to DSS have never been about protecting Addison from an abusive environment."

Mr. Lee arched a bushy eyebrow but remained silent as he scribbled furious notes in his little spiral notebook.

"The first time the allegation was directed at me, and it was declared unfounded. This time, she went after Eli."

"I see. And you are in court now?" Mr. Lee looked up.

Eli nodded. "We won an extended Christmas vacation, and an updated visitation schedule. Tandy refused to cooperate in mediation, but the judge granted our requests."

"But that was months ago," the social worker said.

"Yes, but she wasn't happy about it. I received this from my attorney yesterday." Eli handed over a paper to the social worker. "It's another request to revoke the new schedule."

Mr. Lee looked skeptical but didn't respond.

"I would like to meet your daughter now."

"Of course, we're having dinner with my parents tonight. Please follow us."

The social worker drove behind their car as they

headed to his parents. In the car, Cassie fumed. All attempts at keeping peace with Tandy were over. She was done.

"Tandy will never step foot in my home again, for any reason." She spat the words through gritted teeth.

"Agreed." Eli squeezed her hand. They continued holding hands during the drive. When they arrived at Eli's parents, Eli introduced the social worker.

"Mom, Dad, this is Mr. Lee. He's here to talk to Addison," Eli said.

Linnane's eyes grew wide, but she didn't ask questions. "Addison is upstairs playing with her dolls."

She led them into the dining room, and they took seats at the dining table. A few minutes later, when Addison came down, they introduced Mr. Lee to her. Addison immediately crawled under the table and grasped her grandmother's leg. She refused to come out.

"She's not normally this shy," Eli apologized.

"No, she was full of energy before," Linnane added.

"Give her some time to warm up, and she'll be fine," Bryant said.

"She's just scared," Cassie said. Everyone's attention turned to her, but no one argued her opinion.

For twenty minutes, Mr. Lee asked questions, and Linnane gave him a piece of her mind.

It took Addison that long to come out from under the table. She then crawled into Linnane's arms and talked freely with the social worker. He asked her simple questions, and she answered them. Then he got to the point.

"Addison, I need to ask you about your dad?"

"Okay," she said as she wriggled on her grandmother's lap.

Everyone sat quietly and waited.

"Are you afraid of him when he gets mad?"

"No," Addison said.

"What about when he yells at you?"

"He doesn't yell at me."

"How does he punish you when you do something wrong?"

"We sit down, and he tells me I did something wrong."

"Has he ever spanked you?"

"No." Addison stared at Mr. Lee as she spoke.

They watched as the social worker made more notations in his little booklet and then stood.

"Thank you for your time and your willingness to let me talk to Addison. I'll let you know if there are any further questions."

They had a quiet, subdued dinner after his exit. It was a strange meeting. They hadn't expected to be in the room when he talked to Addison, but he hadn't asked them to leave, so they had sat there in silence, trying to be a calming presence.

The way the investigation was being handled left much to be desired and more than a dozen questions left unanswered.

CHAPTER 16

A Drive through Marriage

Eli

Eli sat next to Cassie in a worn, oversized leather chair across from his lawyer. It was just another day and another depressing visit to his lawyer's office.

The weeks after the visit from DSS had been long and painful. They spread the DSS reports over Chaiken's desk, along with Tandy's second request for termination of Eli's parental rights. Her constant attempts at cutting him out of his daughter's life were wearing him down.

"Are you serious about getting married?"

Chaiken asked from behind his imposing maple desk.

Eli shrugged.

"Somehow, the idea of marriage has lost its spark." Cassie stiffened beside him.

Eli grimaced and patted her hand. *Oh, I'll have hell to pay now!*

"These allegations are a way to get under your skin, and another attempt to create a wedge between you. The fear of not seeing your daughter is a powerful motivator," Chaiken said.

"Well, it's working." Eli gritted his teeth and looked away.

"I have a ring, so I guess we're serious," Cassie said.

Eli peered at her as she looked down at her ring. He loved that ring. It was a four-carat, oval-shaped old mine cut Aquamarine in a beautiful antique filigree setting. He knew it was the one after first laying eyes on it. There was no doubt it added to Tandy's animosity. Her simple gold band was the best he could do at the time. They had been young, broke, and pregnant.

He caught Cassie's glance as she looked up, and he nodded.

"A piece of advice, get married. As soon as you

can. The fastest way to stop her from trying to separate you is to present yourselves as a solid team. Social Services will be less likely to suggest you move out if you are married."

She nodded in response.

"Okay," Eli said, glancing over at Cassie. "We'll do that."

"Will it really make that much of a difference?" she asked.

"There are no guarantees." Chaiken leaned back in his chair. "It is, however, far more difficult to break up a marriage. Last time, her allegation was all they needed for social services to suggest Eli walk away from your relationship."

Eli flinched. He could never make up for the hell Cassie had been through. It would take him the rest of his life to even come close. *If she even gives me that chance.*

At her sharp intake of breath, without turning his head, he gave her a side-eyed glance, to see how she was faring with these reminders of Tandy's crap. She sat stiffly in the chair, staring at the lawyer without blinking.

He sighed. For a moment, he hesitated. *Is it even fair to tie her to me? To give Tandy other opportunities to hurt her?* Was it selfish that he wanted her by his side, regardless of what Tandy threw at them? Or maybe because of it. Cassie balanced him. Made him a better person.

It gutted him that while his life was better because of her; could he really say the same about what he brought to hers?

Cassie sat, leaning away from him. Her hands folded in her lap. He couldn't even reach out and casually hold her hand. Her silence made him feel even farther from her.

"Thank you, Doug. I appreciate everything you're doing. We have a lot to think about."

Eli stood and extended his hand to Cassie. She took it and he helped her up. They walked to the car in silence, though her hand remained in his.

In the car, the silence was killing him. But he didn't have the foggiest idea what to say. He sucked in a deep breath and took a leap of faith.

"What do you want to do?" he asked. He kept his eyes on the road, afraid to see her expression.

"We don't need a long engagement."

"What do you think of eloping?"

"I'm not opposed to it," Cassie whispered.

"But?" He couldn't help it. He needed to see her eyes. When he glanced over, she was chewing on her lip, but didn't seem angry or upset. This relieved him more than he could have thought possible.

"I've always dreamed of a traditional wedding. The billowing white dress, cascading flowers, the decorated cake, family, and friends there to celebrate the day with us. But if you're serious about fast-tracking things, I understand."

"What if we did both?"

Confusion clouded Cassie's eyes as she stared at him. "Both? I don't understand."

"What if, for the sake of the court and the bullshit with Tandy, we elope? Run to a courthouse as soon as possible and get it over with. And have a real wedding with our family and friends as planned, later."

Her entire body stiffened. His heart dropped into his stomach. This wasn't going like he imagined in his head. He was blowing it.

"And your family and their friends would consider that even more excessive," she griped.

"I really don't give a damn what my mother or her snotty friends think about how we live our lives."

She sighed.

His gut clenched even tighter. *Damn it.* This wasn't how it was supposed to be.

"I guess we could make that work," she mumbled.

"I hate to say it, but I think Chaiken is right. This may be the only way to stop Tandy."

"Well, at least your mother would stop nagging about us living in sin."

Eli rolled his eyes. "I'm not concerned about my mother right now."

"Should we have our families there?"

"Why bother? Let's make this about us for a change," he replied.

"If they have a real wedding to fuss about later, they might not mind missing the Vegas-style drive-through version." She shrugged.

"I never thought of it like that. It fits somehow." Eli chuckled. *At least she isn't completely opposed to the idea. Thank god.*

The rest of the drive home, Cassie remained silent and lost in her thoughts.

He ground his teeth. Things were not getting off to the romantic start he'd hoped for. With all of Tandy's drama, it forced him to focus on her, and not on his happily ever after with Cassie. He loved her. She was passionate and funny, and Addison adored her. If Tandy would just leave them alone, life would be fantastic. He deserved that. He deserved a new life with Cassie. Happiness together, Addison did, too.

Eli felt like an ass of the first degree. Cassie never counted on any of this, and yet she'd been right beside him all the way, even through the worst that Tandy threw at them. He didn't deserve her. He really didn't.

A FEW DAYS LATER, DURING THEIR LUNCH BREAK, they met at the city clerk's office with Thean as their lone witness. Cassie had dressed in black wool slacks and an embroidered white V-neck sweater. A pair of black suede pumps, and pearls in her ears, and a single strand around her neck.

Eli arrived wearing a pair of blue jeans, a navy-blue t-shirt, and running shoes. Thean looked the same as they had both come from the shop. Though they were considerably more casual than the event called for, at least they were clean.

Eli caught Thean eyeing him and smirked. The officiant's reaction to their appearance was comical. She looked Eli up and down and then peered at Cassie and back again with the strangest expression. The woman was noticeably uncomfortable with their appearances. The way she stared at Cassie's middle, wondering as if this was a shotgun wedding? Admittedly, they made an odd couple, and Eli couldn't fault her. It was an unusual experience. He never expected to marry Cassie by a justice of the peace, in a quickie-type ceremony without family and friends present. Even his wedding to Tandy had been more than just a single witness and a few repeated vows.

He took her in his arms and turned her to him. "Are you sure? We don't have to rush this." He squeezed her.

"I love you. I'm sure." Her voice held no hesitation. Her eyes were bright and clear, and her smile removed every hint of doubt.

"I love you, too."

"Real wedding still to come, right?" She stared into his eyes.

He held her gaze. "Absolutely."

"Okay, then let's do this."

He leaned over and kissed her. "All right, let's get this show on the road." He hugged her tight, gave her one last kiss, and then slipped his hand into hers as they faced the woman about to join them in holy matrimony.

Less than thirty minutes after they arrived, they

left as husband and wife. There were no flowers, no photographs, and no family. It was as if the day didn't happen at all. Put into motion so fast, he hadn't given Cassie the chance to ask for anything to mark the day by.

After a quick kiss goodbye, they had parted on the courthouse steps to return to work. The reality hit him like a gut punch on the drive back to the shop. They were married, and yet other than a piece of paper, there was little to remember any of it by. Eli should have thought ahead and, if nothing else, brought her flowers. Something to give her a decent memory of what she'd agreed to do, just for him. Because of him. Hell, he hadn't even considered asking Thean for a picture with his phone.

He'd dropped the ball. She hadn't asked for this mess. And yet she'd stood by him and faced Tandy down at every turn. The least he could have done was make it romantic and memorable, instead of treating it as just a formality that held no emotional value.

There would be no chance to get away until after the drama with Tandy was over. But he knew he needed to make this up to her.

.   .   .

LATER THAT EVENING, THEY SHARED THE NEWS WITH Eli's parents at dinner.

"You really did it?" Linnane was incredulous.

"This afternoon. Thean came with me," Eli said.

His mother looked from Eli to Cassie and back. "If it wasn't for Thean being there, I'm not sure we'd have believed it."

"I'm not sure I believe it myself." Cassie laughed.

"Well, it's for the best," Linnane said.

Eli glanced at Cassie and rolled his eyes. He reached for her hand, and she squeezed it, giving him a tepid smile. Leave it to his mother to rain on this moment. There really was no pleasing the woman.

THREE WEEKS AFTER THEIR IMPROMPTU MARRIAGE, Eli sat in the old courtroom and looked around to ease his nervousness. The dated row of wooden chairs was a constant reminder of the folding chairs from high school. They creaked as he shifted in his seat. He reached over and tucked Cassie's hand into his. He gave her a tentative smile; grateful she was beside him. Her love and support gave him strength.

He was tired of coming to court and dealing with the same shit from Tandy. Just the thought of it made fury coil in his gut. He couldn't wrap his head around how he had so misjudged his ex. Everyone he loved had suffered in ways he'd never expected because of who she was. Her vindictiveness had no limits.

"The Family Court of Unity County is in session, Honorable Judge Boozemen presiding," the bailiff said.

The judge entered from his usual door to sit on the bench.

"You may be seated." The sounds of creaking wood filled the room as everyone sat at once.

Eli shook his head. Though he'd been here many times in the past three and a half years, it felt like he was hearing the bailiff's speech for the first time.

When his case was called, he joined Chaiken at their usual table on the right side of the room as Tandy moved to the empty table on the left. Cassie held a vigil in her seat in the front row of the galley.

Chaiken began as though shot from a cannon.

"Your Honor, it's important to understand that

this is not the first false accusation Ms. Heaver has levied at my client and his wife."

Eli snuck a glance across the aisle at Tandy. She glared back. It was clear she wasn't expecting that bit of news.

"Ms. Heaver has also accused Mrs. Tetrick of sexual abuse in the past."

The judge peered over at Cassie as Chaiken continued. "In this situation, just as in the previous case, the investigation absolved both Mr. and Mrs. Tetrick of any wrongdoing. There was never any abuse. This is another attempt by Ms. Heaver to punish Mr. Tetrick and his wife for moving on with their lives by trying to take away his daughter."

The judge put his hand in the air to pause Chaiken's tirade. "Give me a minute to review these reports," he said.

A few agonizing minutes passed before the judge looked up. Staring straight at Tandy, he said, "I see no information here that proves Mr. Tetrick has done any harm to his daughter. In fact, just the opposite."

Tandy looked down at the table, avoiding the judge's gaze.

The judge continued, "I see no reason to

remove Mr. Tetrick's parental rights or change the current order of visitation."

Eli let out the breath he'd been holding and looked over his shoulder at Cassie seated behind him. He bit his tongue, shaking his head in frustration. He tried to be satisfied there were no further consequences for him, but once again Tandy faced no repercussions for her lies.

"Is there anything else for this court to review?"

"Yes, Your Honor. We would like to request the child be sent to a therapist. The continued accusations against my client and his wife make it clear Ms. Heaver has issues that must be addressed. We believe they are affecting the child and her relationship with my client. If there are no objections, we would like to request Sheri Ingram."

"I see." The judge glanced down at the papers again.

The judge glared at Tandy. "Ms. Heaver, I'm going to order the child to go to Ms. Ingram for counseling."

"She doesn't need it. She has no issues at my house. Only Mr. Tetrick and his *wife* say there are problems," Tandy all but sneered.

"I understand, but it won't hurt to have her visit a therapist and get a second opinion."

"Yes, Your Honor." Tandy looked from the judge to her hands flat on the table.

"Anything else?" The judge peered over the rim of his glasses.

"No, Your Honor, that's all we had," Chaiken responded.

"Then the visitation schedule will stay the same and the child will see a therapist. We are adjourned." Judge Boozemen banged his gavel. The sound echoed in the quiet courtroom before the room started buzzing again.

Tandy stormed out without looking back.

Eli stood up and reached for Cassie's hand. She gave him a soft smile, which he returned. They walked out, holding hands behind Chaiken. Once outside, Cassie leaned over and hugged Chaiken tightly.

"Thank you, Doug," Cassie said, as she grasped the lawyer's beefy hand in hers.

"My pleasure," the lawyer said.

"Why didn't we ask the judge for sanctions or penalties against Tandy for lying? This is the second time she's done this. Isn't that illegal?" Eli asked, his frustration growing.

"Yes, but we're lucky the judge left things as is," Chaiken said.

"Why?" Cassie asked.

"Because there's a risk the judge wouldn't see things our way. I was more concerned about keeping Eli's rights intact."

"Bullshit. She got away with this crap again," Eli vented.

"I know. Be patient, in time the judge will see." Chaiken waved at them and then turned right to return to his office a block away.

They crossed the street to their car when a couple of Tandy's friends standing down the street heckled them.

"Hey, dirtbag, I know where you live," a tall, disheveled, waifish woman hollered.

"Yeah, asshole, if you ever touch your daughter again, I'll kill you," a short, obese woman squealed at them.

"You better watch your goddamn back! You too, bitch." The skinny, homely one screamed.

"Back off," Eli yelled.

He ushered Cassie into the car and sped away from the courthouse towards Chaiken's office. Once parked, he took a deep breath before storming into the office.

"God damn it." He cursed in the front lobby.

"Whoa, Eli," the lawyer said, as Cassie walked in the door behind him.

"Hi, Charlene," Cassie said, as she aimed for the desk where Chaiken's wife, who was also his paralegal, sat.

"Didn't you guys just leave court?" Charlene asked.

"Yes."

"I thought it went well? Doug said it was settled."

"It was," Cassie said.

Chaiken stared at Eli. "Eli, what happened?"

"Two crazy bitches threatened to kill us as we headed to the car," Eli responded.

"You need to call the police," Charlene said. Her face mirrored the shock Cassie felt.

"She's right. You should report this at once," Chaiken added.

"Tandy got away with her lies in court. She's lied to everyone, and we're being threatened because of it. This needs to stop," Cassie said. She shoved her trembling hands into her pants pockets.

"Go now and make sure I get a copy for my records in case it continues, and we need to inform the court."

"Thanks, Doug. I appreciate the cool-headed advice," Cassie said, looking straight at him.

Eli lowered his eyes, embarrassed at his over-reaction.

They walked out of the office hand in hand and headed to the police station.

At the police station, the officer in charge didn't seem overly concerned as he filled out the paper-work. It frustrated them no one seemed willing to put Tandy in her place, allowing her to continue to harass them as she pleased. They left the station with a copy of the police report they could fax to the lawyer's office later.

CHAPTER 17

Firework Folly's

Cassie

Cassie took a deep breath of the warm air. She sat watching the waves crashing on the shore, leaving foamy trails in their wake. She licked her salty lips and smiled, thinking of the sands and sea of home. This was their first opportunity to get away since they were married.

They had driven to the Outer Banks the night before, getting in late. The cozy bed-and-breakfast was the ideal place right off the beach.

Their room gave them a spectacular view. They

ate breakfast on the covered balcony overlooking the ocean on a handcrafted teak patio set tucked against the house behind a white painted waist-high banister.

The open air gave Cassie a sense of peace. She missed the sweet sounds and calm of the ocean, something she had frequented often as a child and taken for granted.

North Carolina may be where they lived, but Florida would forever have her heart. Words she would never say aloud. A married woman for three months, her home was supposed to be where her husband and daughter were. But she missed her old life and the simpler times, where there was less drama and fewer people to please.

"What time are we meeting your parents tomorrow?"

Eli looked up from his paper. "Dinner time. Mom suggested Stormy's Place around five. If we get there early, we can have dinner and watch the fireworks from the veranda or the beach. They launch the fireworks right over the water."

"That sounds perfect."

"I told Addison we'd play on the beach this morning after breakfast."

"Let's make it a picnic."

"I'll run to the store and order a couple of sandwiches from the deli and pick up snacks."

Nodding, Cassie sipped her coffee and picked up the comic section Eli had discarded.

After breakfast, they drove to the beach. Eli and Addison played in the water, swimming and splashing before they all piled onto the blanket. Eli handed out lunch.

Cassie propped herself up against Eli and dug her toes into the sand. The further down her toes reached, the cooler the sand was. She unwrapped her roast beef sandwich and took a big bite, before glancing over as Addison picked at her sandwich.

"Are you feeling okay, honey?" Cassie asked.

"I'm not hungry. I wanna make a castle." Addison squirmed and picked up her shovel.

"Wrap your sandwich back up and put it in the bag. You can eat it later," Eli said.

Cassie said nothing, but the frustration over the typical Addison move nagged her. She knew Addison would be hungry later when she wanted something different to eat instead of the healthy food offered. She shrugged it off. *No point bringing it up now.*

Addison scooted off the blanket and sat beside Eli in the sand. She giggled as she turned over different sized buckets of sand in a semi-circle in front of her. With his finger, Eli poked tiny squares holes around the top of the towers.

"There, now you have windows."

"Thank you, daddy."

He then carved an arched opening in the bottom. "And a door." He handed her the small sand bucket and stood. "We need water." He picked up the other two pails, and holding Addison's hand, they trudged to the water's edge. They scooped up water, traipsed back, and plopped down in front of the three towers.

Eli gouged a deep circle of sand out at the base of the largest tower with the little blue spade. He tipped the largest bucket at the edge of the hole. "A moat for the princess' castle."

"Yay, they can go swimming!" Addison cheered.

They played in the sand while Cassie clicked away with the camera. This was their first real vacation as a family, and she wanted to savor every moment.

Just as the wind picked up, and the blue sky changed into the rusty sunset, they called it a day. They packed up their picnic and, while Eli hauled the basket and toys up, Cassie carried Addison to the car.

On the way home, they stopped for an early dinner at a quaint local establishment on the beach close to where they had frolicked. It was a family-style restaurant where everyone shared the same meal. Sitting outside on the patio, Eli flipped open the menu and pursed his lips.

"The menu's pretty simple. There's only a handful of choices."

"What do they have?" Cassie asked.

"Hamburgers?" Addison piped up.

"No honey, sorry, it's all dinners like at home," Eli said.

Addison folded her arms and huffed.

Eli rolled his eyes and turned his attention back to the menu.

"Spaghetti, a pot roast, linguine and clams, a seafood trio that comes with shrimp, scallops and clams, or Swedish meatballs," Eli said.

Addison let out a dramatic sigh. Eli ignored it, and when the waitress came back, they ordered the home-style pot roast with all the sides.

"This is fantastic," Eli said. He speared a mushroom and smiled as he chewed.

"It's almost as good as your mother's."

Eli grinned. "Addy, why aren't you eating?"

"I'm not hungry." Addison moved the food

around on her plate in circles, dragging the meat through the gravy and potatoes.

"Are you feeling okay?" Eli asked, concern in his voice.

"I'm full from lunch."

"You didn't finish your sandwich," Cassie said.

"I ate half."

"Okay, honey, but if you don't eat now, there is nothing at the hotel until breakfast," Eli said.

Cassie remained silent. She wasn't in the mood to argue about food with Addison.

Eli and Cassie made small talk while Addison sat in silence, brooding. She answered when Eli spoke to her, but otherwise remained quiet.

Dinner was pleasant, even without Addison's participation.

"We should take some of this with us for Addison," Cassie suggested.

"No, it will just go to waste back in the room overnight."

As they left, Cassie and Eli talked about the plans for the morning. "I need more film for the camera. Let's go to a quick stop tonight."

"Sure. It's right down the street."

Cassie ran into the store alone. Ten minutes

later, she came out with the film and found the car in a different location.

Pulling the door open, the overwhelming aroma of food filled her nose. A quick glance in the back explained the scent. Addison returned her stare, her mouth full of a burrito from a fast-food place down the street.

"Are you serious?" Cassie looked at Eli as she climbed into her seat.

"What? She said she was hungry."

"We just left the restaurant. She should have eaten dinner with us."

"What did you want me to do, let her starve?"

"How can she be starving when she wasn't hungry some twenty minutes back? And you said not to take the leftovers for her, but as soon as she sees a fast-food stop, she's starving. You've got to be kidding me," Cassie snapped.

"She said she was hungry. I got her some dinner," Eli muttered.

"So, you reward her for not eating her sandwich at lunch and not eating a proper meal at dinner with junk food the first chance she gets?"

"I didn't mean it like that."

"Daddy, do you want some of my soda?"

Cassie stiffened at her needling voice.

"No Addison, eat your dinner. You asked for it and I expect you to eat it all."

"Yes, daddy."

Cassie's jaw clenched. This wasn't the first time Addison had pulled this and got away with it. She was sick and tired of the way Addison manipulated everyone around her to get what she wanted. Everyone pandered to her and coddled her, making sure they met her slightest whim. Eli did it out of guilt for leaving as he did, and his mother seemed to do it out of a misguided attempt to be a more lenient grandmother than she had been as a mother.

How could she convince her husband they needed to be on the same page? If they were to work together to raise Addison, they couldn't be pitted against each other at every turn. It may have been considered a petty requirement that she needed to eat what everyone else ate. But it was more about his daughter adjusting to a routine of family meals. There would be exceptions, of course, but they couldn't cater to her either. While she only wanted what was best for Addison's well-being, she wanted peace and less drama in their home life as well.

Cassie stewed in silence the entire drive back to

the hotel, tuning out the chatter of Addison in the seat behind her and Eli's constant glances aimed in her direction. They were still not speaking when they arrived, or when he carried Addison's sleeping form up to her bed. She showered and crawled into bed with her back to him, still not ready to have the much-needed hashing out that was long overdue.

THE MORNING WAS COLDER THAN CASSIE HAD expected. As she pulled the chair away from the table, she shivered, rubbing her hands over her bare arms. She backtracked into the room for a sweater before sitting to pour a cup of coffee from the thermos pot. The tension emanating from Eli was unmistakable.

They ate breakfast in silence. Cassie savored her quiche while Addison picked at hers. Cassie bit her lip and focused on the comic section of the paper. After showers and breakfast, their first visit was to a lighthouse the OBX hosted.

Addison was perched on Eli's lap during the forty-five-minute ferry ride out to Ocracoke Island. Addison's hair whipped in the breeze. Cassie sat beside them, gazing out to the lighthouse in awe as it grew closer. The ride was turbulent in the choppy water.

"The Outer Banks are known for these magnificent towers," the tour guide said.

Cassie listened, though distracted, as she watched them get closer to the island. Addison fidgeted and wiggled.

"Most lighthouses standing today on the Outer Banks were built in the nineteenth century. The newly formed country, America, found itself in need of a better way for ships to reach the shore safely. Past the sandy banks that protected them."

Eli reached over and clasped Cassie's hand. His touch tugged and pulled as the boat moved.

"Ocracoke is one of the shortest towers at only seventy-five feet and painted a solid whitewash color as a *Harbor Light*, unlike the other four of the 'great five' *Coastal Lights*."

"Isn't the legend of Blackbeard based on that island?" A woman asked.

Everyone turned to face the guide as they waited for her response. Even Cassie's attention piqued at the question.

"Yes, once Blackbeard's favorite hang-out. He perished there in 1718," the guide replied. "There is a pirate museum in the village with stories of

Blackbeard and other pirates of the day." The guide swiveled in her seat, facing the passengers as the ferry skimmed up to the dock. She glided to the exit where a crew tied up the boat.

"Where can we find maps of the island?" a man asked from behind them.

"You can find maps at the gift shop at the end of the dock. They will show you how to find all the sites."

Addison reached for Cassie's hand as they disembarked, the three of them linked as they walked down the dock and into the gift shop. Eli found the maps while Cassie and Addison went to the refrigerated section in search of bottled water.

They spent the day walking around the island following the trail of Blackbeard's footprints, ending at Springer's Point Reserve. An afternoon of sight-seeing left them famished, so they stopped at a pub for lunch.

"Addison, if we order this pizza, you will eat it. You can't change your mind or decide you want something else once it gets here," Cassie said. She glared at Eli, silently challenging him to say otherwise.

"I will." Addison bobbed her head.

"Okay. Just so you understand, there will be no

more of what happened last night. If you don't eat the pizza, there's nothing until dinnertime."

"I know."

"All right, then. Tell daddy the pizza you want."

Eli reread all the pizza choices, and Addison picked one. There was no drama about today's lunch, and Addison ate two slices before she sat back and rubbed her stomach.

They returned to the inn to relax and watch a movie until it was time to meet up with Eli's parents. The three of them piled onto the bed as Cassie turned on the television. Ten minutes in, Eli began snoring. Addison snuggled closer to Cassie and giggled. Within twenty minutes, Addison was slack-jawed and her eyes were closed. Cassie looked over at her sleeping family and sighed. It had been a good day. They'd had a rough start to their weekend, but things had improved.

Cassie fell asleep, a smile on her face.

Showered and refreshed from their naps, they strolled into the restaurant a few minutes early. Eli's parents sat at a spacious table on the patio. Upon seeing them, Linnane waved them over. It was a perfect location to watch the fireworks.

After exchanging air-kissed cheeks, they ordered drinks and perused the menus.

Addison colored on her menu, and placemat while Linnane gave them suggestions based on her experiences.

"Addison, what would you like?" Linnane asked.

"Chicken fingers," Addison looked from Cassie to her grandmother.

Cassie smiled. "Sounds yummy. Are you sure? You know the rules."

Addison rolled her eyes and crossed her arms over her chest. "I know the rules," she huffed. Addison didn't throw tantrums like many children, but her flair for the dramatic was unparalleled.

"If she doesn't like it, we can always get something else," Linnane said.

"No, Mom. Addison needs to eat what everyone else eats or what she asks for," Eli said. Cassie glanced at him, grateful for his support. She didn't want another night arguing about Addison's eating habits.

"She's a child," Linnane scolded.

"So was I, and you would never let me get away with that crap," he said. "Addison will not become picky or hard to feed."

Linnane glowered at Cassie but kept her opinions to herself. Cassie was sure there was a scathing rebuttal itching to come out of her mother-in-law.

They enjoyed dinner with minimal gossip. As they dug into dessert, the fireworks lit the sky.

Eli and Brian stood at the banister and had a beer. When the dishes were cleared, Addison crawled into Cassie's lap and settled. She wrapped her arms around Addison and hugged her close, letting her chin fall to Addison's head as they pointed at the fireworks' reflections on the water.

CHAPTER 18

A New Adventure

Eli

E li took the morning off for Addison's first day of kindergarten to walk her into her classroom with Tandy. Tandy kept to herself, and Addison seemed content. On one of her visits, she admitted Luke moved out over the summer and filed for divorce. The girls were told not to speak his name at home. Within a few weeks, they learned Tandy was dating again. It was no surprise. She wasn't known for letting the grass grow under her feet where men were concerned. For all concerned, life had been quiet.

Eli had asked Cassie to join him the night of Addison's school's open house. It was important that he attend, but he admitted he didn't want to go alone.

A few moments after they arrived, Eli nudged her. When she looked across the room, she saw Tandy standing with her back to them, with the two girls between her and a broad-shouldered man. Though she shouldn't have been, it surprised Cassie to see Tandy's new boyfriend there at the school for Savannah and Addison's open houses. He carried Quinby's infant seat and stayed with Savannah during the entire event. Whenever he was near, Addison seemed to distance herself from him, standing alone a few feet away. They wandered around the halls, looking at the various finger paintings on the walls and such.

"Missing Savannah's first steps into school still haunts me. I never got to experience any of that with her. I wonder if there's any chance I can sneak over to take a peek at Savi's classroom as well?" Eli whispered.

Cassie squeezed his hand. "Go to the bathroom and get lost on your way back. I'm sure I can distract them if I have to."

Twenty minutes later, Eli had gone to the men's

room to scope out a way to check out Savannah's work without causing a scene. Addison and Savannah played on the swing set outside. Walking over to the bench where Tandy watched the girls from, Cassie decided it would be a good idea to bridge the gap since they would be in each other's lives for the foreseeable future.

"Would you mind if I sat with you for a moment?" Cassie asked.

"Sure." Tandy continued to stare at the play area.

Addison smiled and waved in their direction, and Cassie returned Addison's wave and smile.

"I'm sorry to hear about Luke."

Tandy did a half shrug.

"I'd like to make peace."

"Okay." Tandy turned to face her.

"I'd like to put the past behind us and move forward." Cassie slipped her hands under her knees to stop the fidgeting as her stomach did nervous flips.

"I'd like that too." Tandy gave her a tense smile.

"I'm glad to hear it. For Addison's sake." Cassie let out a deep breath.

The two girls continued to play on the swing set

a few feet away while they sat in silence, watching them.

Eli came out of the classroom and called out to the girls on the swings. "Hey girls, I need to leave now. It's getting late."

Addison jumped off the swing and came trotting up, with Savannah close behind.

"Okay, Daddy. I'm glad you came." Addison hugged him.

"I love you, bugs."

"Love you too."

Savannah had stood a little off to the side, and when Addison took a step back, Eli reached out and took Savannah's hand. He gently pulled her into an embrace.

"I love you too, Savi," he said. He kissed her cheek and stood.

Tandy was standing a few feet away with a man holding a baby seat.

"Eli, this is my boyfriend, Rafe," Tandy said.

Eli reached out and shook Rafe's hand. "It's nice to meet you. We were just leaving."

Cassie stood and moved beside Eli. No one had bothered to introduce her. She nodded at Tandy and Rafe. Without another word, they left.

When the car exited the parking lot, Eli glanced at her. "He was an interesting-looking fella."

"Was it the shaved head, or the violent and graphic tattoos?"

"Where does she find these guys?"

"Let's not forget you were one of them once."

"Oh please, let's." Eli grinned.

"Eli, why didn't you introduce me to Rafe?" Cassie asked.

Eli's head swiveled to look at her. "I'm sorry. I honestly didn't even think. I just wanted to get away from her. Them. I guess. I should have. I'm really sorry." He squeezed her hand as his attention moved back to the road.

"It's okay," Cassie whispered.

It broke her heart that she still wasn't in the front of his mind. *Will I ever be the first thing he thinks of?* They drove the two hours back to Durham, listening to an audiobook, engrossed in their thoughts.

CHAPTER 19

A Small Step Forward

Eli

Eli sat in court beside Cassie, wishing he was anywhere else. Kindergarten began at the start of August, and they hadn't even made it to Thanksgiving before they were back in court again. All attempts at civility had failed over the last few months.

The kindergarten teacher called Eli about Addison's constant absences. She was under some strange impression that he controlled her attendance. Only Tandy had that. He hadn't known about most of the missed days unless they coincided with a missed weekend visit. Addison rarely told him when she didn't go to school. Both her attempts and the schools frustrated the teacher to reach Tandy and come to an understanding.

The room quieted, and they called the court to order as Judge Boozemen entered, and the bailiff ordered everyone to take their seats. The judge looked frustrated; his expression was ominous. The frown on his face was severe, almost like he had no lips left.

There were three other cases reviewed before it was Eli's turn.

Chaiken and Eli sat at their standard table as Tandy sat at hers. Cassie remained seated in the first row behind Eli.

"Your Honor, my client has concerns about Addison's well-being in her mother's home and the lack of communication between him and Ms. Heaver."

"I've given *him* everything he needs to know," Tandy interrupted. Her arms folded across her chest, she glared at him at the table across the aisle.

The judge peered over his glasses at Tandy, and she pressed her lips together. He returned his attention to him and his lawyer.

"Ms. Heaver has tried many tactics to prevent

Mr. Tetrick from seeing his daughter," Chaiken said.

"I have not…" Tandy erupted from her chair.

The judge swung his head back to her.

"Ms. Heaver has made accusations against Mr. Tetrick and his wife. Unfounded sexual abuse, and physical abuse, and when that didn't work to stop the visitations, Mr. Tetrick's weekends are canceled because of illness. He would miss out, sometimes not seeing his daughter for a month at a time," Chaiken continued.

"What are you asking for?" the judge asked.

"Mr. Tetrick would like provisional orders set up. We have no alternative but to ask this from the court in the event there is a problem. If the child is sick, there are no exchanges of weekends or substitution options available. The orders are straightforward. These are his weekends and those are hers. If your honor will simply read the case history, Ms. Heaver has made him honor all her time with the child. It's only fair Mr. Tetrick gets that same consideration."

"Your Honor, it's unfair to force my daughter to visit when she is ill. She needs to be at home with her mommy so I can take care of her," Tandy said.

With the way the judge narrowed his eyes at

Tandy, his lips in a thin tight line, it left little doubt the guilt trip wasn't working.

"We would like to request a revised visitation agreement that missed visits be made up," Chaiken continued.

"I agree with Ms. Heaver."

Eli's shoulders slumped at the judge's statement.

"The child shouldn't be forced to go anywhere when she is sick. She should stay home with her mother."

It deflated him as his chin dropped to his chest for a moment before he looked back up at the judge.

The judge lifted his hand in a stopping motion. "However, if it occurs, the visits are to take place the very next weekend regardless of earlier plans, unless a mutual agreement is made."

"Thank you, Your Honor," Chaiken said.

The breath Eli had been holding escaped.

"Ms. Heaver, more communication with Mr. Tetrick might keep the two of you out of court."

"Yes, Your Honor."

Tandy's voice was low and didn't hold the usual arrogance he expected from her. He wished he could believe that this meant she'd be more cooperative. As they walked out of the court, Eli rolled his eyes and sighed.

"I can't imagine what the difference is between which parent takes care of Addy when she's sick. It's not like I'm completely inept here."

"I know, Eli, but at least we've ended another one of her games. One fight at a time, that's all we can do."

Eli nodded and reached for Cassie's hand. Another day lost. Another fight barely won. He was just so tired of it all.

REGARDLESS OF THEIR PRIOR MINI VICTORY IN court, Cassie wasn't the least bit surprised to find them in Chaiken's office three months after their last court date. Though Addison's weekend visits improved, her school attendance did not. The teacher continued to call Eli weekly, and communication with Tandy had deteriorated further.

"Eli, it's time to consider asking for full physical custody."

Cassie glanced at Eli and held her breath.

"Doug, that's crazy. I can't take Addison away

from Tandy or her sisters," Eli said as he turned to face Cassie.

"Why now?" Cassie asked.

"Tandy is hell-bent on hurting you through Addison. Unless you do something extreme in response, her games are not likely to stop."

"Seems over the top, though. There has to be another option."

"Under the circumstances, this is what I recommend." Chaiken lifted his hand in the air and ticked off Tandy's actions on his fingers.

"The abuse accusations she threw at each of you, her continual excuses preventing visitation weekends with Addison. Not to mention her antagonistic behavior hasn't ceased."

"I agree, it's gotten worse," Eli said.

"Think about it. Tandy does as she pleases. She's never held accountable for her actions, short of your divorce from her," Chaiken said.

"Yeah, I know."

"And I don't see that changing."

"I don't understand. How does asking for full custody stop Tandy's games?" Eli asked.

"Simple. It's all about perception."

"Perception of what?" Eli asked.

"Of you. Right now, she sees you as unwilling

or unable to fight back. She's got you by the balls, afraid of losing Addison–like you lost Savannah–you are more controllable. She knows you're less willing to make any waves of your own."

"That's true," Cassie said.

Eli stared at Chaiken without responding. His expression remained stoic, but his face had paled.

"I know it's a lot to take in. Please give it some thought. You don't have to decide anything right this minute," the lawyer said.

"Thank you. We'll call you." Cassie rose and shook Chaiken's hand.

Eli hadn't moved. He continued to sit frozen, looking at the lawyer.

Cassie rested her hand on his shoulder.

Eli shook his head. "Yes. Sorry. Thank you, Doug." He scooted his chair back and reached across the desk as he stood.

"We'll talk soon."

Eli nodded, and Cassie followed him out. The ride home was quiet and when they got home, Eli headed for the shower. When she went to ask him about dinner, she found him fast asleep, his hair still damp. She covered him with the blanket and kissed his cheek. He was in for the fight of his life, and he was going to need all the rest he could get.

CHAPTER 20

What Makes A Mother

Eli

Eli still struggled with asking for custody. The thought of pulling Addison from the only home she'd known tore at him. But each time she visited; her stories became more unsettling. He'd even talked to the therapist a few times about some things Addison said.

The therapist, while bothered by the way Addison was being isolated by not attending school regularly, was most disturbed about the violent arguments between her mother and Rafe, Addison described witnessing.

He had hoped for a more definitive suggestion from the counselor, but she'd only relayed a few of the conversations she was concerned about and left off giving him any proper direction.

Cassie had been his sounding board over the days following the meeting. He wavered and waffled, and then would decide, only to change his mind again. It wore him out.

Eli appreciated how supportive Cassie was, but she continued to ask him tough questions. This would not be a simple fight, and it would get nasty before it was over. He needed to be solid about his decision before he began.

They had dinner with his parents that weekend to discuss his feelings. Sitting at the table, Eli explained the situation.

"You will need to follow your gut, son," Brian said.

His mother wasn't nearly as receptive. "This is wrong, and you shouldn't consider this path."

"Mom, I have to do something." Eli shook his head.

"Children belong with their mother."

"Do you think this is easy for me?" Eli snapped. "Seriously, mom, you've seen for yourself what Tandy has done. Do you really think she was in the right with false abuse charges? Why aren't you as incensed as we are? All I've ever wanted was a relationship with my children that did not include drama from Tandy. Instead, she's fought that with every step. Damn it, she's kept Savannah from me and now trying to keep Addison from me, too."

His father put a hand on his mom's arm to stop her from saying anything more, but the tension in the air was miserable as they finished dinner in silence.

The plates cleaned and the wine glasses empty, Eli followed his father outside to the garage. He needed to get away from his mom before he really exploded on her. He'd never felt this hurt by his mom. Her lack of support on this important issue caused his stomach to swirl with bitterness. He resented that his family, when he needed them the most, wouldn't stand behind him.

WITH THE MEN OUTSIDE, CASSIE REMAINED IN THE kitchen, helping her mother-in-law clean up after dinner. The tension pulsated between them, so Cassie remained silent while she cleared the table. Linnane stood at the counter, rinsing off the dishes and putting them in the dishwasher. Her back was to the room, and her shoulders were stiff, so Cassie avoided bringing other dishes to the counter until she cleared everything else.

"You don't understand because you're not a mother. Maybe someday you will when you and Eli have a child," Linnane said.

A chill ran down Cassie's spine as she stood there, staring at the back of Linnane's head as she paused with an almost empty wineglass in one hand and the bottle of wine in the other. The words were as painful as if someone had dumped a pile of bricks on her. Her chest constricted and her eyes welled with unshed tears.

"You're too hard on Addison," Linnane continued.

Cassie sucked in a breath and, with a shaking hand, poured a little wine in her glass and gulped it. If she was honest, she was an inch away from chugging directly from the bottle.

And you let her get away with murder. You are the one teaching her to be manipulative and demanding, just like her mother. How is that a good thing?

Her mother-in-law's rebuke stung, but something told her this was deeper than a mere difference of ideology; she didn't understand Eli's mother at all. She poured another glass of wine, this time to the rim, hoping to fortify herself.

From the beginning, Eli's mother had criticized her about everything, from living with Eli before they got married to her parenting style. How many times had she heard things like, *your expectations of Addison are too high?* How many times had she bitten her tongue when Linnane admitted to being a strong disciplinarian with Eli as a child and often the things she criticized Cassie for, she was herself guilty of.

"You don't show any patience for Addison when she's with you."

Wow, this coming from the woman who often chased Eli around the house wielding a wooden spoon. Eli was full of stories of his childhood with his parents' strict, rigid parenting style. Apparently, they had mellowed with age in an ironic twist.

"I've been more than patient, not only with Addison but with Tandy as well, all while making sure Eli and I aren't further hurt," Cassie muttered into her glass.

"You don't give her enough freedom to be a kid," Linnane continued.

Eli hadn't been allowed to watch most cartoons because you disapproved of their content, even without watching them.

"Freedom?" Cassie choked. "Because I won't let her run around other people's houses like a wild animal, because I'm trying to teach her manners and respect... because I care enough to see she grows up knowing right from wrong?"

Linnane shook her head. "When you have children of your own, you'll see what I mean."

How could she be so clueless? Her grip on the wine glass tightened. Frustration filled her to the bone. She found Eli's mother condescending and hypocritical, considering how she'd raised her son.

"I only want what's best for Addison," Cassie said.

"Yes, but there's a bond that exists from birth. Parents love their children."

"Are you saying I don't love Addison? Because *that* is not the case."

At Linnane's bland expression, Cassie continued. "Of course, parents love their children, but parents also have a responsibility to provide more than a bohemian existence."

"I didn't mean it like that," Linnane's voice was stiff, contradicting her words.

Cassie worried they would never have a comfortable relationship. The constant disapproval emanating from their interactions was exhausting.

And once again, Linnane condemned them for trying to do what Eli thought was in Addison's best interests, based on her bias.

"Children belong with their mothers, regardless of the circumstances. You and Eli have no business trying to change that," she added, her attention trained on the dishes in the sink.

"Are you serious? She's lying to the courts. She's creating reasons for Eli not to see his child. Regardless of what you think of me, you should care about what she's putting your son through."

"I do care," Linnane said.

Why was Eli so afraid to ask her to back off? She has no idea what we're going through.

"I really can't imagine how you could stand there after everything that's happened and still support Tandy instead of your own son, who only wants to protect his daughter." Cassie grit her teeth before she exploded further.

"Look, I understand why you feel the way you do. But the bottom line is, Tandy is her mother, and I don't want to lose my granddaughter. If I support this, Tandy will keep Addison away from us, as well as Eli. She's already done that with Savannah, and I can't lose another grandchild. I'm sorry."

"I can't believe this. So, Tandy can do whatever

she wants to Eli? To Addison? As long as it doesn't affect you. Got it. Nice to see where you stand. No matter your opinion of me, you know the truth. There's no excuse for putting your head in the sand, pretending Addison isn't being hurt by her mother's actions," Cassie said, anger lacing her words as she stormed out of the kitchen. She was done. *God, there isn't enough wine for this shit.*

She couldn't remember a time when Linnane had been supportive of anything about her. Her opinions, where Eli's ex-wife and daughter were concerned, continued to widen the gap between them. Sometimes, Linnane was a one-woman sabotage tag team against them all.

She's so damn frustrating. Even the truth, when faced with it, changed nothing. *So much for happily ever after.*

Becoming the evil, wicked, step-mother, and hated daughter-in-law had not been in her plans, nor could she have expected to feel as isolated as she did.

I just don't know if I can do this anymore. Or if I want to. Is this what I really want?

Cassie sat outside on the front porch with her glass of wine and the empty bottle and stewed while she waited for Eli to take them home.

—————

THE FOLLOWING DAY, CASSIE TOOK A QUICK BREAK to check emails before her last meeting of the day. It amazed her how much spam and advertisements she accumulated each day. Her inbox would no doubt explode if left to its own devices. She shook her head at the number of new messages and took a sip of her now warm soda, the ice long melted. *God, I really hate Mondays.* The dinner with her in-laws the night before nagged at her. She wished it had gone better.

There was a new email from someone she didn't recognize, but the name was familiar. Clicking on it, a note from Eli's aunt filled her screen. Eli's mom must have given her Cassie's email address. Their family weekend was coming up in two weeks. They would head down to Florida and spend a couple of days with her parents before meeting up with Eli's family. It would be the first time she would meet most of Linnane's side of the family. Considering the tension with Eli's mother, she wasn't looking forward to the trip.

From: Sabine Stephens

To: Cassandra Tetrick

Subject: Wedding Registry

Cassie,

You can go online to the gift registry and do your thing. I didn't try it out, but you should.

Are you ready for our little reunion?

"NOT ANYMORE," CASSIE MUTTERED AS SHE continued to read.

I probably shouldn't stick my nose into this, but I want to help with my sister. Linnane said you two were constantly butting heads, and she doesn't know how to make it better.

Cassie laughed. That was an understatement if there ever was one.

Her and I butt heads often, but always make up. I love Linnane dearly. To understand her, you must know it's her compassion and generosity to her family and friends that drives her. If you feel smothered by her, or she's doing too much and always involved in your life, you're so lucky. It's hard to take sometimes, but Linnane loves you and cares deeply, and she would never want to hurt you.

Maybe a nice lunch date where you two can talk alone would help. I'm sure Linnane would love to clear the air.

Cassie sighed. She'd tried to clear the air with her mother-in-law, but Linnane only heard what she wanted to hear. If she didn't agree with something, she tuned it out. She kept reading.

I never got along with my mother-in-law. I wanted to, but to her, I was never good enough for her little boy. She always complained to my face about my makeup and how I looked. Went through my cupboards complaining about how I spent our money. She was just awful. We never developed a relationship. It's rather sad. It would have been nice to have another mother to cling to. I can't help thinking of you and Linnane and hope you can have the wonderful, close relationship I missed.

I apologize for sticking my nose where it doesn't belong. Linnane would like her relationship with you to be better. Her heart is heavy. Every relationship requires some give and take. I hope you see Linnane differently now. Don't for a moment think she's against you. Best of luck, it takes time to build good relationships.

Your concerned aunt,

Sabine

CASSIE SIGHED AS SHE RELAXED INTO HER CHAIR. She was grateful Sabine had reached out to her because it was important to mend things with her mother-in-law, but was she in over her head? She only made things worse whenever she tried.

Linnane's disapproval was stronger than ever.

This was ironic, since she hadn't particularly liked Tandy, and they hadn't been close at all. But because she was the mother of Linnane's only granddaughter, Linnane turned a blind eye to Tandy's drama, not to mention the lies and accusations she flung out. Cassie's frustration with her mother-in-law was reaching an all-time high.

Even Eli had agreed they needed space from his parents.

He'd called her at lunch to tell her he'd talked to his mom, and it hadn't gone well. His mother blamed her, of course, which only fueled the fire and infuriated him more. By the time her lunch was over, and they hung up, he was angrier than he'd been in months.

It hurt her heart to see the distance between his family, with his daughter. It felt like everything was spinning out of control and she could do nothing about it. But there was a small part deep inside her soul that was grateful that he'd stepped up to his mother and finally told her how he felt about her interference and lack of support. Now it was in her hands to figure out a way to mend things with her son. It wasn't Cassie's place to, and she had no desire to even try.

From: Cassandra Tetrick
To: Sabine Stephens
Subject: Wedding Registry

Hi Sabine,

Thank you for reaching out. Linnane's disapproval is more about her desire to have things her way, and only her way. She steamrolls over anything she disagrees with, regardless of why. I'm exhausted. I'm trying to be a good wife and a good step-mother, but I'm up against Eli's ex and his mother at every turn. The battles are heartbreaking and infuriating all at once.

I'm giving us both space before the relationship deteriorates to the point of no return, and sadly, that is the path it's on.

Can't wait to meet you in person.

Love,

Cassie

CHAPTER 21

Are We Twins?

Cassie

Three days had passed since she'd shot off a quick response to Eli's Aunt Sabine, so it pleased her to see a reply in her inbox. Cassie sent the message about the changes to her ongoing project, then opened Sabine's email. It felt rather cloak and dagger to have these conversations with her husband's aunt, considering they had yet to meet. Cassie had not mentioned the first email to Eli, though she wasn't sure why.

From: Sabine Stephens
  To: Cassandra Tetrick
  Subject: I understand

Cassie, I understand your situation. Linnane does not share all the details, and I don't ask. She has, however, shared a lot of wonderful things about you and believes you are a great person for Eli.

CASSIE SNORTED. THIS WASN'T HER EXPERIENCE. While Linnane wasn't hostile, she wasn't encouraging, either.

Linnane's ability to forgive and forget so fast can be a problem. I can't remember a time where Linnane has ever stood her ground and kept it.

Cassie nodded as she read this email. Sabine seemed like she'd noticed the same things she had. It was good to find someone who could relate.

Linnane doesn't pay attention to details. She lets herself get wrapped in everyone's sad story.
  As far as Tandy, Linnane never said anything good about that girl. She's up to no good, and she doesn't trust her, but Linnane gets wrapped up in it, and usually ends

217

up in trouble. Linnane believes she's helping you guys, but she needs to butt out until she's asked for help. I told her the same.

She wants to be needed. She loves Addison, sometimes too much if that's possible, but I'm not there to see how things are. I'm only cognizant of what she tells me, which isn't much.

Don't give up on Linnane; she has a heart of gold. Linnane and Brian spent a lot of money and time bailing out Eli and Tandy with all kinds of problems. Linnane will soon see you are not Tandy, and you can manage things. Time always helps.

Well, hang in there. I know what you're up against and it is possible to work them out.

I'm glad we talked, Cassie. I've enjoyed getting to know you and hearing your views. I do think we'll get along just great, as none of my siblings are like me, in any way, shape, or form. I love them all, but you know what I mean. It will be great to have support with you there.

Have a great day,
Aunt Sabine

From: Cassandra Tetrick
To: Sabine Stephens

Subject: I understand

Thank you for the insight into Linnane. It's been hard, but you are right. She needs to be needed and has been a stable influence in Addison's life since she was born, so I'm sure having me do things differently drives her as crazy as she drives me.

I'm looking forward to getting away. I miss the beach so much.

Love,

Cassie

CASSIE DASHED OFF A QUICK RESPONSE. SATISFIED IT was safe, politically correct, and wouldn't offend, she logged out of her email. It was good Eli's aunt understood her, even if his mother didn't have a clue. For the first time since beginning her relationship with Eli, she just might have found an ally. That was a strange feeling.

Not wanting to be late meeting her girlfriends, she grabbed her purse and headed out the door. Drinks with the girls turned into dinner, and she didn't make it home until late. Eli was dead to the world when she slid into bed next to him.

The next morning, she was exhausted. During the drive to work, she'd drained a large cappuccino. She grabbed another from the cute little cart in front of the lobby on her way up. If nothing else, she'd be fully caffeinated.

Cleaning out her voicemail took a few minutes. It was the usual stuff. Nothing urgent needed her attention. She pulled up her email and settled in for the day. There were two hot-button issues she needed to deal with first, but they were simple enough to answer.

Caught up in her thoughts, the jangling of the phone startled her. Shaken out of her reverie, she recognized the number and picked it up on the second ring.

"Hi Tamsen, how are you this morning?"

"Good, I made my flight. I'm in New York now, but I wanted to check on you since we stayed out late last night."

"Yes, I'm still trying to wake up."

"You sound distracted."

"To be honest, I am. Eli's aunt has been emailing me for the last few days."

"About what?"

"Well, the family reunion and the tension with Linnane."

"Oh, boy." Tamsen let out a long sigh.

"No, it's been good. She's not bashing me at all. It's a pleasant change to have someone who doesn't think everything I do is wrong."

"I'm sure it is. Being a newlywed is hard, but being a newlywed and a step-mom is the worst."

"Seriously, why is that?" Cassie asked, fiddling with the pencil on her desk.

"Girl, if they told us the truth, most of us would have run away screaming and changed our numbers. No one intentionally signs up for this crap. We're in love and optimistic, but once the ink is dry and we can't get away, the ugly truth rears its head."

Cassie snorted, a very unladylike sound, as she laughed. Tamsen could make any situation less tense. It was one of her favorite qualities of her college roommate.

"Thank you for that," she said.

"I aim to please." Tamsen giggled. "Anyway, I just wanted to make sure you were okay and tell you I made my flight."

"I hope to see you soon."

"You will. Bye for now."

As Cassie set the phone down, she picked up the printed emails from Sabine. She would tell Eli about them when she got home to get his opinion on them. It might surprise him to learn someone else understood her issues with his mother. She wanted them to get along, but she also wasn't a submissive doormat that didn't speak her mind.

CHAPTER 22

A White Wedding

Cassie

Cassie fidgeted in her chair, the tension in her shoulders fierce. More than half a year had passed since the day they'd run to city hall and gotten married. They had about one week to go before their actual wedding. So far, their efforts to keep their arrangements quiet had been successful in avoiding further drama from Tandy.

Her parents flew up for the weekend for the final wedding preparations that included appointments to pick out tuxedos. Though Tamsen couldn't make it down from New York, Thean's wife, Hannah, Enaria, and Cassie's mother, Claire, would help with the final details after lunch.

"Cassie, are you sure this is the right thing to do?" Claire asked. "First, you fast-tracked the marriage, and now you're having this big wedding and keeping it such a secret." Her mother's piercing gaze seemed to see right through her.

They were in a quaint little teashop, taking a moment to relax while the men shopped for groomsmen gifts after the tux appointment.

"It's complicated, but considering Tandy's reactions to us, we figure the wedding wouldn't go over well if she knew. Besides, it's none of her business, and if we let it slip to Addison, she'll know at once."

"I understand. As much as I like Eli, I can't help wondering if marrying him was the right choice."

"Mom, now you're sounding like Linnane," Cassie groaned, "I love him. We hope things will die down since there's no chance of breaking us up."

"But you're already married. I don't understand why it matters to keep the wedding a secret." Claire leaned in closer.

"Mom, every time we take a step forward in our life together, Tandy retaliates in some horrible fashion. She's always making excuses about Addison being too sick for visits. She wouldn't hesitate to cancel her visit the weekend of the wedding to spite us."

"What does the lawyer say?"

"He's working on it being addressed next time, but until then, we avoid unnecessary drama."

"How are you keeping it from Addison?"

"On the rare weekends Addison is with us; we focus on spending our time together. We agreed to not discuss the wedding in front of her. Whenever she asked, we tell her it's after the holidays."

"What about her dress and shoes? How will you get them to fit her?"

"A friend got married over the summer and used Addison as her flower girl. We bought her a dress and shoes. We just bought them a little bigger in case she had a growth spurt."

"That's smart. You've thought of everything."

"We tried. I always wanted my wedding to be a big traditional production. Eli didn't, considering it was his second. It's a compromise."

"Was it Eli's decision to cut the guest list?"

"Yes, just immediate family and our closest friends."

"Well, the Historical Society in Chapel Hill is the perfect venue."

"I'm glad it will be outside. That was all I really wanted. I've always dreamed of my ceremony being held in a garden. We're having it on the terrace. It's in the back, facing the lawn and the lake."

"With the weather being so persnickety up here, I hope it doesn't rain."

Cassie nodded.

Armed with a printout of a dozen styles she wanted to see; they spent the rest of the day at the bridal salon trying on dresses. They had ordered the bridesmaid dresses online months before. Now Cassie needed to find hers. It was a fluke when the sales lady suggested the one on display in the front window and that it had not been the stark white color she'd been trying to avoid. It was nothing like she expected to wear, yet it was perfect. Her dress had found her.

THEIR DAY WAS FINALLY HERE. AFTER EVERYTHING that had happened, Cassie was getting her white wedding and her happy ending. When they arrived at his parents, Addison got swept up in the excitement. Friends and family had been streaming in and out of Eli's parents' house for days leading to the wedding.

The morning was a blur of activity. Too much for her to even try to keep straight. Linnane had taken over doing Addison's hair and makeup with a little gloss and blush, and a shimmering body spray.

Tamsen, Enaria, and Hannah, Cassie's three closest friends, were bridesmaids. The girls had all taken part in putting Cassie together.

Even with others giving her a hard time for spending money on a wedding, this day had made it all worth the efforts. She wasn't nervous at all. The normal anxiety and fears new brides experienced were absent. Then again, it could be because it felt right. Though it had been a whirlwind romance, her heart overflowed with love for Eli. And her gut told her she was exactly where she was meant to be.

Walking down the aisle on her father's arm, he matched her steps to keep her from a face plant that would have happened without his support. The three-inch heels were already making her self-conscience.

The pale champagne tinted A-line dress swished around her legs with each step. The delicate embroidered sequin lace covered the bodice, in a V-neck over her shoulders into three quarter length flutter sleeves, and covered her entire back in lace. Her sleeves brushed against her father's coat and tickled her arms.

She grinned as she peered at Eli at the end of the aisle, waiting for her. The ceremony passed in a flash, and the next thing she knew, Eli was escorting her into the banquet room.

Brightly colored bouquets filled the room. In the center, tall sunflowers nestled in vases, surrounded by morning glories. White calla lilies, ocean breeze orchids, velvety red roses, burgundy tulips, and bold orange zinnias decorated every table.

A hand-blown glass orb filled with flower petals, multi-colored crystals, and ribbons graced the top of the elaborately decorated two-tiered cake.

Being in Eli's arms, Joe Cocker's voice filled the air with *Up Where We Belong*, a song that suited them more than she ever thought possible. She rested her head against his chest and let his heartbeat soothe her as they swayed to the music.

As the music changed again, Eli handed her over to her father in a smooth transition. *Landslide* by Fleetwood Mac played as her father took her into his arms.

After a few beats of the song, the DJ picked up the microphone.

"Can we have all fathers, and their daughters, join the bride and her father on the dance floor?"

Eli and Addison were the first to join Cassie and her father, followed by a dozen of their friends and their daughters.

As the sun dipped behind the horizon, filling the sky with vibrant streaks of color, Cassie gathered the single women and tossed her bouquet into the lively group.

Cassie and Eli laughed and waved at the remaining guests, tossing birdseed into the air, and cheering as they passed through the line of guests to the waiting car.

Come what may, they were taking their first steps toward their happily ever after starting now.

I WANTED TO TAKE A MINUTE TO THANK YOU FOR taking the time to read **His Heart's Burden**.

I hope you enjoyed **Eli and Cassie's** *story. If you did, I would greatly appreciate you leaving a review on the platform of your choice.*

Reviews are crucial for any author and a line or two about your experience can make a huge difference in helping other readers find this book.

DID YOU LIKE THIS BOOK? THEN YOU'LL **_LOVE_** THE first story in the The Letting Love In series **_Her Guarded Heart_**.

Check out **_Her Guarded Heart's_** blurb below.

She's never put herself first. Will the distance she craves only bring her more heartbreak?

NORTH CAROLINA, 1999. ADDISON TETRICK LONGS to escape her mother's expectations. Caught in the middle of ugly custody battles, she's determined to claim her independence. So when an opportunity arises to study in Russia, the college student jumps at the chance to find her true self.

Doing her best to resist her French flatmate's attempts at matchmaking, Addison relishes her newfound freedom. But just as she's finding her feet, a blossoming romance with a handsome classmate and the inevitable pull of family back home place her squarely at an impossible
crossroads…

Can Addison overcome her fears and emotional baggage to live her dreams?

In a story that covers continents, life lessons, and broken hearts, author Dawn Baca weaves a compelling account of how circumstance and personal history can both conspire to emerge as pivotal moments. Readers will love following Addison's journey as she begins to comprehend who she is in the world—and perhaps be inspired to open their own souls to possibilities.

Her Guarded Heart is the vivid first book in the Letting Love In women's romantic fiction series. If you like soul-searching quests, multicultural settings, and touching love stories, then you'll adore Dawn Baca's coming-of-age adventure.

Also by Dawn Baca

WOMEN'S ROMANTIC FICTION

The Letting Love In Series

- **His Heart's Burden** — (*books2read.com/ HisHeartsBurden*)
- **Her Guarded Heart** — (*books2read.com/ HerGuardedHeart*)
- **Her Heart's Desire** — (*books2read.com/ HerHeartsDesire*)
- **His Hearts Promise** — (*books2read.com/ HisHeartsPromise*)
- **Her Heart's Wish** — *(Coming Spring 2026)*
- **Her Heart's Secret** — *(Coming Spring 2026)*
- **Her Lonely Heart** — *(Coming Winter 2026)*
- **His Forgotten Heart** — *(Coming Winter 2027)*
- **Her Fighting Heart** — *(Coming Winter 2027)*
- **His Racing Heart** — *(Coming Winter 2027)*
- **Her Jaded Heart** — *(Coming Winter 2027)*

Contemporary Romance

- **Windswept Whispers** — (*books2read.com/ WindsweptWhispers*)

Holiday Stories

- **Merry and Bright** — *(Coming Winter 2025)*

International Cozy Mysteries
The Travel Visa Mysteries

- **Betrayal by the Bay** (Book 1) — *(Coming Summer 2025)*
- **Ended on Easter Island** (Book 2) — *(Coming Summer 2025)*
- **Suspense on the Serengeti** (Book 3) — *(Coming Summer 2025)*

ROMANTIC FANTASY

The Changeling Chronicles Trilogy

- **Beyond the Veil** (Book 1) — *(Coming Summer 2026)*
- **Whispers of the Fey** (Book 2) — *(Coming Summer 2026)*
- **The Feyborn Legacy** (Book 3) — *(Coming Summer 2026)*

Acknowledgments

Words could never convey the depths of my gratitude. To my amazing beta readers, critique partners and editors, some, who are not only fantastic friends but also amazing authors in their own right:

Amabel Daniels, Becky Austin, Bonnie Phelps, Deb Julienne, Diane Wiggs, Elsa Bayley, Michelle Remy, Michelle Read, Rachel Lamb, Rebecca Snider, and Lorraine Upton.

Thank you to Sherry Franssen Breinig for reading this story more times than I'm sure you would have ever wanted to admit. Your suggestions made this book everything I could have asked for. I miss your great insights every single day.

About the Author

An insatiable reader of all genres since her childhood, Dawn is a globetrotter hungry to discover new places and experience unique adventures.

She can be found indulging in her husband's first love of summer camping in the mountains or luxuriating in the open seas while cruising to exotic destinations during the frigid winter months.

When she's not jet-setting she can be found in Central Valley California with her family and their many rescue animals.

To read her blog, get the latest news, future release dates, or to join her ARC team sign up for her newsletter at *www.DawnBaca.com.*

Social Media

facebook.com/DawnMBaca

x.com/BacaDawn

instagram.com/dawnbaca

bsky.app/profile/BacaDawn

tiktok.com/@bacadawn

youtube.com/DawnBaca

pinterest.com/dawnmbaca

amazon.com/author/dawnbaca

bookbub.com/profile/dawn-baca

goodreads.com/dawnbaca

Paperback ISBN: 978-1-7329615-4-8
Cover: 100 Covers
Editor: Deb Julienne
Chapter Image: Black eyed susan flowers 13243339@Pngtree

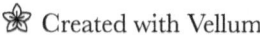 Created with Vellum